BIG SMOKE

THE APOCALYPSE VIRUS TRILOGY BOOK 1

R.F. BLACKSTONE

SEVERED PRESS
HOBART TASMANIA

BIG SMOKE

This is for Mapi, always a believer.

CHAPTER ONE

It's not the wind that makes it cold. Nor the snow. But a combination of both. Then add the altitude. Blowing at well over eighty kilometers an hour, kicking up snow and small pebbles, the sort that at that speed hit one with the force of a punch.

Christine Moore winced at each tiny hit. It hurt but kept her mind from wondering. Plus the view helped.

Snow as far as the eye could see. Desolate and yet gorgeous.

The wind made Christine shift her feet. Digging into the snow further. Behind her goggles, her eyes scanned the horizon. She was starting to get nervous. A quick look at her watch forced her to take a deep breath.

"They're late," she said to no-one in particular.

"Calm your tits," a voice crackled in her ear. "They'll be there."

Christine shook her head. Her gloved hands pulled a scarf away from her mouth. She took another breath, held it for a moment, and then slowly exhaled.

Her breath formed a veil of steam and as it faded into the ether Christine's eyes locked onto four dots speeding towards her.

Eventually, the sound reached her. Snowmobiles. All being revved to the point of no return.

Amateurs, she thought as the mechanical roar of the mobiles echoed around her.

They came to a sliding halt, kicking up snow. Christine smiled, ignoring the cold dampness which splattered all over her legs.

"Sorry 'bout that, luv," the leader said as he galloped off his vehicle. Removing thick goggles, a silly beanie and a ski mask revealed a scoundrelly handsome face.

"Don! Fucking great," Christine muttered to herself.

"C'mon then, show us your face."

She forced a fake smile as she removed her own facial gear. Thick luscious lips, long blonde cascading hair and smoldering eyes that burned deep into him. Don smiled broadly as his men looked her up and down, admiring her curves.

"Hello, Christine! Been a while," he said instantly turning on the charm. "I'm surprised they sent you on suc—"

"—Got it?"

Don laughed and gestured to one of the other men who held up a small metal case.

"Open it."

Another gesture and the goon opened it, reached inside, and pulled out a small thumb drive.

"There," Don said, "happy now? I mean, the last time we met, you were nowhere near as bossy... Well, except for at that bar in—"

"Here." She threw a small sports backpack to him.

Don caught it easily, then lazily handed it to another goon.

Taking the drive, he looked at it. "Such a fuss over this? Amazing."

"Hand it over. Now," Christine ordered with the air of someone needing to get the hell out of there.

"Not just yet," Don said as another gust of wind whipped up even more snow. He coughed as some hit his face. Christine laughed slightly then shifted her feet, loosening the snow around her legs.

"Check it," Don said casually to the man with the backpack who nodded then slowly unzipped it. As he did, the line attached to the zipper triggered the claymore.

The man exploded in a shower of snow and blood, spraying everyone with the vile mixture.

Christine used that moment of confusion to grab the drive and then haul ass.

The explosion had knocked the remaining men to the ground.

They all sat up, slightly dazed, staring at the crater and the smoking wreckage. Surrounding the perimeter was a halo of blood.

Don looked around, coughing and wiping the entrails of the dead man off of his clothes. His eyes flashed as he turned to the remaining goons. One pointed and his eyes followed; there was Christine, blowing a kiss as she skied away.

"Get after her!"

#

Christine stared at the thumb drive then casually pocketed it. Don was right; so much fuss. She chuckled, dodging the trees with ease. Her skiing was always good, but since the incident, it had improved. Free time does that. She laughed victoriously as the wind kicked her hair up around her face.

"Rank fucking amateurs," she said to herself.

But, Christine had to admit it to herself, the operation had gone off without a glitch. Station Master would be proud.

A tree became riddled with bullet holes as she passed, shattering her thought.

A quick glance behind her and the smile disappeared.

There were the three snowmobiles, and the men all had Uzi Pros aimed at her. Each one squeezed the trigger of their weapon.

Christine dodged the bullets easily.

She raised a hand, giving them the finger with a grin.

The men were amazed at how easily she spun, turned, and then disappeared down a pass.

"Follow her," Don screamed as his snowmobile veered away.

Down the mountain pass, swerving this way and that, bullets whizzed past her head. Christine was having a blast. The danger aroused her in such a way that reminded her of Havana.

The trees were coming up fast. *Good*, she thought. Now she had the advantage. The snowmobiles would have to split up. Perfect.

She leaned forward, speeding up, then just as she passed the tree-line, one of the goons squeezed off a few rounds. A smattering of small dead animals fell from the trees, littering the way.

"Damn animals," the goon said as he scanned for the woman.

Unfortunately, he missed the low-hanging tree branch that smacked him in the face. His head snapped backward, body following until the snow-covered ground caught the now limp body.

The snowmobile came to a halt, bumping a tree. Snow fell, covering it with a light dusting. She slid to a halt, kicking up more snow. Then quickly she turned and then headed back to the snowmobile. Christine grabbed the weapon and spare clips from the body, then went over to the vehicle. She kicked off her skis, glided onto the seat, checked the starter, and then before taking off, she put her hair in a pony-tail and hit the throttle.

The last goon spun around, listening for any other gunshots, or man-made sounds... Nothing.

There!

Christine sped towards him, Uzi Pro raised, steady arm.

Shit!

He followed her, constantly firing, forcing her to the left. No matter what Christine did, she had no way to go except left.

"Need an escape route," she yelled into the air.

Her earpiece crackled with slight radio static. She ducked then quickly rubbed her ear. That did it!

"South!"

"No go. They're driving me left."

"Give me a mo'."

More bullets whizzed past Christine's head. The thug was close now. No more tree cover. In fact, there was hardly any cover left.

"Give me a route!"

"There's a cliff coming up." No apology, just a matter-of-fact statement.

Christine grunted as a bullet grazed her arm. "Thanks."

"See you soon."

The radio static ended just as a barrage of bullets destroyed the chassis of Christine's snowmobile. It sputtered then spun out.

Her timing was impeccable, waiting for the moment, squeezing the trigger. The man's head snapped back, the left eye exploded as the bullets shredded the bone and brain, leaving nothing but a bloody pulp.

The snowmobile rolled, hit a rock, then flipped. The body was flung away as Christine smiled.

Her vehicle though kept on spinning. There was a boulder straight ahead. She muttered an oath under her breath and then leaped just as both collided. Christine rolled as the snowmobile exploded, showering her in debris.

"Bugger," she said, dusting herself down and wincing. Her shoulder stung and instinctively Christine knew there would be more bruises and most likely scratches and grazes. *Great*, she thought as she rubbed her shoulders gently.

"Christine, we've got a Harrier inbound."

"Lovely. ETA?"

"Ten. Best we can do."

Christine chuckled nervously, thanking her dumb-fucking luck, as she looked at the carnage surrounding her.

The snow got kicked up. Her hair blew around her face in a tempest. This was not from natural weather. She spun around, looking for the source of the disturbance.

"You've gotta be fucking kidding!"

The Apache helicopter hovered above the wreckage, Don waving at her happily inside. Christine stared at him, dumbfounded. Don pressed a button and a loudspeaker crackled, coming to life.

"Hand it over, Christine. You've got nowhere to go."

Christine slowly started to back up, inch by inch. Her eyes darted this way and that, looking for any escape. The Apache dipped forward ever so slightly, the rotor blades dangerously close to the ground. The death machine started to approach her. Don smiled and it seemed as if he was humming a tune.

Christine Moore raised her arm, the Uzi pointing straight ahead. Slowly, her finger squeezed the trigger.

She emptied the clip at the helicopter. Don reacted without thinking, flinching as the Apache darted to the left, the blades hitting the snow.

That's what she was waiting for. It was now or never.

As the helicopter straightened itself, she ran full speed directly at it, her hands moving fast, reloading the Uzi.

Christine dived under the aircraft, unloading the clip into the belly of the metal beast. The clanging echoed around the mountains. Some of the bullets ricocheted back into the snow around her. She continued to run under and out, behind it.

The Uzi did nothing to the metal underside.

"That wasn't very nice," Don's voice sounded as the Apache turned to face her.

The Gatling on the snout started to rotate.

Christine waited, watched, made ready for the only move she had left.

The .50mm caliber bullets spewed forth, tearing the landscape a new one. She stood there, her training paying off.

A lovely trail of bullet holes spattered around her, but she did not flinch one inch. Then as the weapon slowed to a halt, Christine ran, back towards it and the cliff.

She threw the gun to the ground and grabbed the only thing she had: A pickax.

Don stared in amazement. Did she really think that that would do anything against an Apache? She must be crazy.

But Christine knew exactly what she was doing. As the helicopter dipped again, ready to lop her head off, she dropped onto her back, sliding towards the edge.

Over she went.

Plummeting into the abyss.

She slammed the tool into the rocky cliff-face. It scrapped and slipped as gravity and her weight pulled her down towards oblivion.

Then it bit, catching a small outcropping.

The sudden stop flung her out and then her body slammed into the rock wall, hard. So hard in fact that Christine almost lost her grip. Her other hand snapped up, grabbing the handle, then using her legs, she supported herself while figuring out the next move.

"Now what, sweetheart?"

Christine sighed, not even bothering to look at the helicopter hovering in front of the cliff and her helpless self.

"Give it up. Tell you what," Don said into the loudspeaker, "you climb back up, hand it over, we call it even. I'm sure Station Master would appreciate another chance."

Christine chuckled and then held out one hand, flipping Don the bird as she relaxed her grip. As she slid, she muttered, "Awwww fuck it!"

Don's smug look disappeared as Christine Moore plummeted into the bottomless emptiness.

CHAPTER TWO

"Come," Station Master's voice bellowed.

The large oak door opened. Christine entered, nodded curtly to the old man who ran The Station, walked over to the middle of the room, and stood. Station Master had aged since the last time she had met with him. There were more wrinkles and liver spots but less hair. What hair was still there had been styled not in a comb-over, oh no that would be against style, but slicked back in that timeless style. The old eyes were a little glassy, but that comes from age. Station Master was bent over the wooden desk that dwarfed him, both hands on the ink blotter, his eyes darting back and forth across a file.

Christine could not believe that he still used paper files.

"You can stop staring, Miss Moore," Station Master said without looking up.

"It's been a while Station Master."

The old man sighed; it was long, seeming to escape from within him. "Did you get it?"

Christine smiled as she laid the thumb drive on the table. Station Master's eyes darted up, first to the device, then to his agent.

"Any problems?"

"Ran into an old friend. Nothing I couldn't handle though." She allowed herself a small secret smile at that.

Station Master chuckled, "Oh yes, how is Don Hanscomb?"

The smile faded from the blonde's face. *How did the old goat know?* she thought to herself.

"It's my job to know; you should remember that."

Christine shifted, slightly uncomfortable at the jab. "Naturally, Station Master... Drink?"

He waved to a bar that was perfectly ordained with the proper glasses, a tantalus filled with the golden liquid of ancient and ambrosia-like whisky, which was sitting against one of the walls. Christine went over, bent slightly, and searched for the right bottle.

"Behind the Makers. I'll have mine without anything sullying it."

Christine chuckled as she found the bottle, Havana Club, judging from the label it had to be at least pre-Castro. The cork popped, the sound filling her ears with memories, then she poured it, the gold-amber liquid filled the glass. "Two fingers?" Station Master mumbled his answer. Christine poured another glass then took them back over to the table.

"Such a fuss for that little thing, eh?" she said as she handed the glass to her superior, who ignored the remark.

"Christine," Station Master began, "do you know what it is that The Station does?"

The woman shook her head as she sipped the rum. She held in a little sigh of happiness. "All the jobs that the other agencies don't want, or can't do?"

Station Master took a drink from his glass, coughed at the remark, and nearly dropped the glass. He was laughing as he cleaned himself up. "Not exactly. But close. As always. The Station is in the darkest recesses of the clandestine world. The Dark Web is our best friend. The Black Market, an uncle. We go and do what the others will never do..." he looked at the thumb drive then out the window. The view was dank; thunderclouds, sleet. Truly unpleasant. "But now," he continued, "with the state of the world, our small part is being annexed. So, what must we do?"

Christine's eyes were now focused on the thumb drive. It was sitting between them, silent yet screaming. "What is on that?"

Station Master reached for it, his old fingers having trouble grasping the device. Christine watched; age is a harsh bitch.

"This?" the old man said, holding the drive up. "This is the next evolutionary step."

He tapped a button and the ink blotter flipped, revealing a

control panel. He inserted the drive into it and a screen appeared behind him.

"What, my dear, can you tell me about President Aaron Sanderson?"

As he spoke, a dossier of Aaron Sanderson appeared on the screen.

"He's the current president of the USA," Christine said as she refilled her glass. "On paper, and on-screen, he is perfect."

The president's image was that of an old matinee idol. Perfect hair, cleft chin. Everything the voters of the USA wanted.

"Squeaky clean?" Station Master asked.

"Squeaky fucking clean. On paper and screen. But..."

The old man raised an eyebrow; go on, it seemed to say.

"But," Christine said as she leaned against a wall, her eyes staring at the dossier, "by all accounts, once he is out of the spotlight, the real Aaron Sanderson appears. Bigoted. Misogynistic. Uncouth. Completely barbaric."

"What about his wife?"

Christine laughed, a harsh bark. "A trophy wife who does exactly what he says or else the money runs out. Ex-strippers tend to be like that."

Station Master sat there, his eyes sparkling with contained glee; *the young and foolish,* he thought. "What about his politics?"

"His platform is to make the USA spectacular. And to do that, he plans to fuck everyone over...the world over." Christine's eyes narrowed. There was only one reason for this line of questioning. "Spill it, old man," she said. "What's all this about?"

"Intel, Miss Moore. We have valuable intel." He pressed some buttons and a map of a small island appeared. "Surely you recognize this place?"

Christine nodded, her mouth wide open. "Cuba."

Station Master nodded. "Very good. Tell me about the Habanos Festival."

For the briefest of instances, Christine's lip trembled and her mind raced trying to ignore the painful memories. Finally, "It's five days of nothing other than smoking Cuban cigars, drinking Cuban rum, and partying. Habanos S.A., the governmental body that controls all the cigar industry there, runs it. Apart from being a damn fine party, it provides extra money for the coffers, advertising for tourism in Cuba, and naturally, it reestablishes the age-old idea that Cuban cigars are the best in the world."

Station Master watched her. "Is it true?"

She shook her head. "I use to think that, but…not since…"

The old spymaster nodded.

They drank in silence, she lost in memory, he studying the woman before him.

"The intel says that there will be an assassination attempt on President Sanderson. In Cuba. During the festival."

"What?" It took a brief moment for Christine to focus on what the man had said. "Why is the president going to the festival? The president of the USA has never…" She stopped, thinking. "The embargo!"

Station Master nodded, then moved around from behind the table. His wheelchair moved silently, gliding him across the room. Christine watched; she couldn't remember the last time he had done this, as he took her empty glass then over to the bar, where he refilled both.

He motioned for her and they stood in front of the window, staring out at the water. The storm raged on. "Fitting. Isn't it?" he said as he handed Christine her glass.

"What is?"

He sipped, the gold liquid burning his throat slightly. "It's always darkest before the dawn. The coming storm. Take your pick."

"Station Master?"

The old man sighed then turned his gaze from the weather to the woman next to him. "You fucked up, young lady. This is your chance."

"For revenge?"

"No," Station Master said, shaking his head. "Redemption. Consider this your moment for resurrection. Think Lazarus, rising from the dead."

Christine lowered her eyes, briefly avoiding the gaze from the old man. "So what? Stop the assassination?" Station Master nodded. "But," Christine continued, "who would want Cuba to stay as it was?"

"Only one name has been mentioned in all the inter-agency chatter. Jeremiah Banks."

Christine didn't say a word as she drank the rum. Station Master watched her.

"Is it really him or just chatter?"

"Since the talks between Cuba and the USA started up again, there has been word from that organization he runs. His syndicate. But he hasn't shown his face since you were last there."

Once more, the woman lowered her head. She asked silently for forgiveness knowing full well it would never come. When she looked up, her eyes were steely and her jaw set, resolutely.

"Give me the mission, Station Master."

The old man smiled, not fatherly but smugly, then raised his glass. "Christine Moore, go to Cuba, stop the assassination attempt of President Sanderson, bring to justice the party responsible for this plan and," he paused then grinned, "if you just happen to run into Mister Banks, why not send him our best wishes."

"Only if," Christine said with a sly grin. Both chuckled as they raised their glasses.

"To Cuba," Station Master toasted.

"To second chances," Christine muttered under her breath as they drank.

#

The parcel was small, the size of a camera bag. Christine hated when Station Master sent her these "gifts" as he called them. She opened it then slowly took out the contents. Inside was a passport, an airplane ticket to Cuba, and a reservation confirmation for a hotel. *That'll have to be changed*, Christine thought. There was only one place for her to stay in Cuba. Also included were the dossiers for Sanderson, Jeremiah Banks, the Habanos Festival, and the head of Cuban Intelligence.

And there was a note from Station Master:

Miss Moore,

Failure to complete the mission is unacceptable.

If you are unsuccessful, then might I suggest retiring somewhere far away.

Somewhere without Internet. Or cellular reception.

But, if you do succeed, then your Mission Status will be changed from LIMITED to ACTIVE.

Good hunting, and don't fuck this up.

"I love you too, Station Master," she said as she eyed the intel about the festival. Her mind swam, memories of Havana creeping in. Memories of her.

Christine shook her head. *This is how you failed last time*, she thought, *letting yourself get caught up*. She had a job. The mission was all that mattered.

She couldn't... No... *Wouldn't* let anything get in the way of the mission.

Not the past.

Not Jeremiah Banks.

Not even Adriana Prado.

CHAPTER THREE

The flight from Cancun to Havana was smooth. In fact, for Christine, it was downright dull. The landing was a little more exciting though. The tires screeched, the back end of the plane spun out, but luckily the pilot was good. When the plane came to a stop, he came over to Christine and apologized for the rough landing. He added, just before Christine stepped down the gangway, that he hoped Station Master would use his service again.

Christine shook her head, the poor fool, as she went through customs and immigration. José Martí airport had changed since the last time she had visited. Once where people could easily pass through without being hassled, now there were state-of-the-art body scanners, facial recognition systems, and the best passport scanners. *The benefits of US Dollars*, Christine thought as she headed for the exit.

Outside, the sun hit her, followed quickly by the sea breeze and all the smells. She smiled, feeling at home. She looked around; all the taxis were busy, picking people up, dropping off. There was a line at the taxi stand. She snorted; *no time for that*.

As single gringo men and boys stared in wonder at all the pretty Cuban señoritas, Christine placed her single piece of luggage down on the ground, adjusted her skirt slightly, then raised her arm. The effect of her legs and cleavage showing caused a taxi to nearly crash into a bus.

"Welcome to Cuba, señorita," the taxi driver said as he paid off the bus driver. He took her bag, swiftly put it in the trunk, then held a door open for her. As she climbed into the cab, he took a quick glance at her and liked what he saw.

"Muchas gracias," she said as the car pulled into traffic.

"You speak Español?" the driver asked with slight surprise. Christine nodded with a smile; she always enjoyed surprising men.

"Poquito. My Español is a little rusty." It was coming back to her, slowly. By the time she arrived at the hotel, she would be back in the swing of things.

"You speak it very well."

Christine laughed. "Gracias, señor. Dime, how goes things in Cuba?"

The taxi swerved, barely missing a nun, who turned and started to shout curses at the speeding vehicle. The driver laughed as Christine held in a snort of her own laughter.

"Muy bien, but, señorita, a donde?"

Christine cursed herself for not saying that in the first place. "Hotel Nacional, por favor."

The driver nodded as the taxi turned down a side road.

"So?" Christine asked, her Español indeed coming back.

"Cuba?" asked the driver. "Ah, she will always be the same. The gringos came before, tried to make her their bitch. It didn't work then."

"Now, though?"

He laughed. "Nunca, my dear. No matter how much money gets thrown around here, Cuba will always be her own. It didn't work when the Spaniards came. Nor for the gringos. The Mafia? Ha! We took care of them... But, sometimes I'm not sure. When the President... What was his name?... Obama! Si! That was him. Well, anyway, when he started talks with Presidente Castro... The good one, mind you." At this, he laughed again, steering the car with ease, like he had been driving all his life.

"What's wrong with them?"

The driver's eyes glanced quickly at the sidewalk next to the street they were currently cruising along. Christine was staring at the people littering it. They were obviously malnourished and needing to see a doctor.

"The homeless," the driver said. "They always look like that." The man snorted as his eyes went back to the road.

Christine continued to gaze at the poor and needy of Havana. She had seen this sight before, sure; go to any bustling city and the homeless will always be there. What made her stare was the glassy eyes of the children.

Each one had sunken eyes and pale, pale skin. Their little heads were covered in bald patches and the open sores on their arms, legs, and faces oozed blood. Christine's mouth dropped open as a stray dog approached a small boy. The beast sniffed around him and then, after making a decision, it opened its jaws. The fangs pierced the flesh and blood spurted over the beast's fur. Which a quick shake of the head, the boy was on the ground. The dog lunged and started ripping the flesh.

The car turned a corner, but Christine was picturing the jaws tearing into the small body, rending flesh from bone, lapping up the spilled blood, and generally feasting.

Christine shuddered when she realized that there were no sounds. No screaming. No snarling. The attack had happened in complete and utter silence. At least a moan or groan should have been heard. But nothing? Not even the other people tried to do anything about it.

"What's happened to Havana," she asked no one.

"Every few years, the poor get sick," the driver answered sagely. "In the end, it helps us all."

He may believe that, she thought, *but no matter how strong a sickness is, it cannot render someone catatonic.* She once more shuddered at the image of the child.

"Put it out of your mind, señorita."

Easier said, Christine thought. They continued on in silence. Christine now stared at the roofs of passing buildings. She could not remember seeing that sort of thing before. Truly, it troubled her.

How far had Cuba fallen?

What other nasty surprises laid waiting?

Why didn't she get booster shots before flying?

These thoughts and more flashed through her mind. She furrowed her brow slightly and opened her mouth.

A dog ran across the street, forcing the man to slam the brakes. Christine had to prop herself up to stop from being injured.

"Pinche perro," he exclaimed. The beast glanced at them, wagged its tail, then continued on his way.

"Gotta love the wildlife here," Christine said slyly.

"Perros are my favorite. My wife keeps saying that if I had the money, I would get an estate and then save all the poor fellows," he said as they continued. Christine enjoyed the drive. It gave her time to get reacquainted with the city she had spent five years in. This was her home.

"Anyway," the man continued, "since the talks started again, Business Big... Is that how they say it? It doesn't matter," he said before she could correct him. He switched from Español to English halfway through his sentences. It was slightly annoying. "Business Big started buying buildings, hotels, you know... Trying to get as much as they could before the embargo went down."

"How wrong they were, eh," Christine chimed in with a knowing smile.

"You know Cuba well," he said with a chuckle. "And now, Presidente Sanderson is here. For the festival they say. Aye por favor."

They were now driving along the Malecón, the strip of road that also had the famous sea wall. The waves were crashing against it, almost welcoming Christine back. She sighed happily, watching the people smoking cigars, the old men playing dominoes, and the bands practicing.

"...a day into the festival," the driver's voice brought her back, "and there has been no talk about why he is here. Some say, well, you know what they say about rumors?"

Christine nodded. "Do not repeat anything you would not sign your name to."

The driver nodded, sagely. "Well, I would sign my name to any of the rumors about President Sanderson."

Christine looked out the window. In the distance, she could see the twin copulas that were the trademark of the grand dame of Cuban hotels, the Hotel Nacional. She smiled, happy to be at her home away from home. A pause at that thought, and Christine realized something. The Nacional was her home. The only real home she had ever known. And she was ecstatic to be back.

"Señorita?" The driver had stopped to let a passing marching band go by. "I think you have been to my city before. Si?"

"Once," she said, letting the music wash over her. "A long time ago. She hasn't changed."

The man laughed. "Gringo dollars have tried. But she may change her appearance, but, believe me. Habana's soul will always be hers."

Christine nodded as the car continued. "The festival this year. Will it be big?"

"It is the biggest one yet!" The driver seemed genuinely surprised as the old hotel grew closer. "A day already in and there are more turistas here than ever. It will be a spectacular miracle you'll get a room."

"A day already?" Christine cursed her luck. Why did Station Master wait for so long before sending her? A day late, who knows what she had missed.

"Si," the driver said, "but, no sign of Presidente Sanderson. The Battle for Cuba's soul has yet to begin."

The car turned and there they were, in front of the Hotel Nacional.

CHAPTER FOUR

The perfect example of history in Cuba, the Hotel Nacional is the most iconic hotel in the country. The twin cupolas are like sentinels. The rooms reek of the stench of history in each. Old world charm and new world decadence abounds. Built in 1930, surviving wars and revolutions to the renovations in 1992, this is THE hotel in Havana. From Winston Churchill to Frank Sinatra to Jean Paul Sartre to Alexander Fleming, she has seen it all. Only standing eight stories tall, she is not that imposing. But the beauty comes from the history and her character.

Christine knew all this, and more. For the five years she had lived in Cuba, her room had been the Errol Flynn suite, where the famous actor and lover had spent many nights entertaining the local ladies and his special guests. She loved it. Everything was paid for by The Station. But now, she wasn't sure. A more spartan room was called for, though she hoped that Rafael Cienfuentes, the manager she knew, was still there.

"Muchas gracias, señor," she said, paying the man then giving him a healthy tip. He beamed at her, then quickly pulled back out into traffic.

Christine Moore took a breath, gripped her bag tightly, then walked back into her old life.

\#

Inside the hotel was all a hustle and bustle. Christine had forgotten how it got when the festival was on. So many turistas; most of them gringos. She could tell from the shorts, socks with sandals, and the fanny packs. Tacky. Every one of them had cameras and were taking photos of the old guns that were once part of the Santa Clara Battery, which now stood in the garden. She shook her head at them. They all came for the same reason: cheap cigars and lots of attractive women looking for an easy escape. It made her sick.

Then she felt it. The sweat and dirt from the years of being exiled. *Right*, she thought, *first things first; check in and then to one of the two pools.* She needed a swim anyway.

At the front desk, the young lady gave her a snooty look. Christine hated that look.

"Si, señora?"

"Hola." Christine flashed her most lovely smile. "My usual room, por favor."

The lady looked her up and down, sniffed, then, "And does señora have any other baggage? Or a reservation?"

"It's a spur of the moment decision. My room, por favor."

The lady looked around at all the other guests. Her face said it all: you have got to be fucking joking. "Perhaps señora has not noticed, but we are slightly busy at the moment. If señora had made a reservation, then… but…" She raised her hands.

Christine was getting agitated. She wanted to reach across, grab this pendeja by the hair, then pull her across the large desk, slam her onto the floor, and then proceed to give her the beating of her life. But she couldn't. So she didn't.

"May I speak to the manager?" was what she said instead.

The young lady blinked. "Perdon? The manager?"

"Si," Christine said, her voice now tinged with anger. "Get him. Now."

She gulped; obviously, this girl had never had her small amount of authority questioned before. But she bowed her head slightly then disappeared into the back room.

Christine waited. Her nose twitched, the familiar smells hitting her. Rum. Cigars. The sea. Damn, she had missed it all.

"…you are paid to take care of the customers," the deep voice was saying as the girl reappeared, followed by an older man, still young but the gray at his temples told all of his advancing years. "If you can't handle one cust…"

Christine smiled broadly at the man who had stopped dead in his tracks. Rafael Cienfuentes could not believe his eyes. "Hola, you old pervert," Christine said with her arms ready for a cuddle.

He engulfed her in a bear hug. "Señora Moore! I don't believe it," he said as he released her. The young lady behind the counter gulped; she knew she was in trouble.

"Believe it," Christine said. "I need my room."

Rafael frowned slightly, his mind worked. "Señora Moore—"

"—Christine."

He blushed slightly. "Christine, you may have noticed that we are quite busy."

She nodded then took his arm. "True, but," she lowered her voice conspiratorially, "this is business, not pleasure."

Rafael laughed. "It is always pleasure with you, my dear lady."

Christine couldn't help but join in. "True, but I DO need my room."

"Now that," he said with the shake of his head, "is something I cannot do."

She pouted. "En serio?"

The manager nodded. He looked around at all the turistas. He barely hid his contempt for them. "Uno momento, por favor."

Christine watched as he went over to the desk, grabbed a tablet, and then went to work, checking all the rooms and the guests in each. He bit his lip as he did. Christine held her breath; she didn't have a backup plan if the Nacional was fully booked.

Then.

"The Sinatra room," Rafael said to the young lady. "Señora Moore will be staying in the Frank Sinatra room. 225."

"But, what about the guests already there?"

The old manager stared daggers at the young lady. "Kick them out. There have been noise complaints about them. Invite them to leave. Now."

He turned back to Christine, a big smile on his face. "Please forgive us this imposition."

"There is nothing to forgive," she said, giving him another hug.

"Why don't you go up to the rooftop bar for an hour or so? I'll escort you to the room when it is ready. Si?"

He held out his hand and Christine nodded as she handed him her bag.

"That would be perfect."

Rafael nodded with a slight bow. "Once again, welcome to the Hotel Nacional de Cuba."

#

"Un mojito, por favor," she said to the attractive barman, who nodded with a smile and then set about making it. Christine watched intently, hoping that the man knew his job. A perfect mojito is hard to find, but in Cuba? That was the real test.

According to La Bodeguita del Medio, the birthplace of the mojito, this is how to make one:

Take one and a half ounces of Havana Club Rum. Mix it with half a teaspoon of sugar. Then add the juice of half a lime. Followed by adding one sprig of mint and muddle it until you can smell the mint. Add some ice cubes, then fill the glass with mineral water. Lastly, mix well.

Which is exactly how the barman made it. He handed her the glass with a wink, waiting for Christine to taste it. She took a small sip, closing her eyes, enjoying the flavors once more.

"Todo bien?" he asked.

"Oh, si," she answered with a smile. She handed him some Cuban pesos then went over to a chair and table.

The view from the top of the Hotel Nacional was always beautiful. Christine had to admit that. Every time she saw it, it took her breath away.

The rooftop bar was a newer addition; it had brought in more customers to dance the night away. And since the Habanos Festival was in full swing, there were plenty of people up here even though it was midday. She looked at them all, young men and women, older married couples trying to regain their past, and those looking for a good time. She smiled slightly as she sipped her refreshing beverage.

The Caribbean Sea was peaceful, the waves lapping gently against the Malecón. The sounds of it mixed perfectly well with the Cuban jazz band playing all the classics of the Buena Vista Social Club. Christine tapped her foot in time to the music.

If only she had a cigar... Her preference used to be the Trinidad Vigia, one of the best short Cubans in the world. But now she preferred the Nicaraguan Drew Estate Undercrown Shade. But, you get what you can get.

Once she got settled, then it would be time to work. The pool would have to wait. First on Christine's list was to make contact with Cuban Intelligence. She had been out of contact with the happenings of CI, who was in charge, and what they were up to.

"Damn you, Station Master," she muttered to herself. He had sent her in completely unprepared. Yet, that was his way. Every mission was a test, testing his operatives' abilities to operate under these circumstances to see if they were capable. But a little bit of information would be helpful.

"C'est la vie," she said, saluting the city.

"Señora Moore," Rafael's voice cut through the noise. "Your room is ready. Please follow me."

#

"Back to work, I see," the old manager said as they rode the elevator.

"Always and forever," Christine replied. She was anxious to see the room that the famed boozer had once stayed in. "Please tell me something, Rafael."

The man nodded.

"Is Juan still the head of Cuban Intelligence?"

Rafael feigned ignorance. "Whatever is that? Here in Cuba, our government is as open as any."

They both laughed. Christine always liked the Cuban sense of humor.

"Come now," she said, "you wouldn't think me a fool? The Station knows all about that little side job of yours." Christine gave a knowing smile while the manager looked around uncomfortably.

"Forgive me, Señora Moore," he stuttered as the doors opened onto the art deco floor. He held the door open for the lovely lady. "You must understand that in Cuba one must find all the money."

"Relax," Christine said with a laugh and a nonchalant wave of her hand. "You, dear friend, are far too important. Now, which way?"

She followed Rafael as he said, "As far as you are concerned, Christine, Juan de Dios is not of importance." He stopped in front of an old-looking door. Next to it on the frame was a plaque. Inscribed was FRANK SINATRA SUITE.

"Then what is?" she asked with a raised eyebrow.

Rafael smiled as he unlocked the door. "Why, getting to know Cuba again!" he said and with a flourish the door swung open.

#

In keeping with the hotel's style, Art Deco ran through the rooms. Elegant and subtle. Golds with splashes of reds. Christine nodded with a small smile. "Better than I'm used to."

Rafael chuckled as he handed her the key. "You haven't been in Cuba lately."

She shook her head as her eyes spotted a welcome. Bottles of Havana Club Rum Añejo 7, a humidor filled with Trinidad Vigia cigars, Coca-Cola, limes, and a small envelope. Christine pointed. "What is that?"

"That?" Rafael ignored the envelope as he opened the curtains. Sunlight engulfed the room. "That was delivered while we organized your room." He looked around the room, proud of his work.

Christine was staring out the window, her eyes on the waves. In her hand, fidgeting with it, was a cigar. "At least gringo dollars haven't reached you," she said quietly.

"Not yet," Rafael answered quietly as he started for the door.

"Rafael," her voice stopped him in his tracks. He turned slightly, on the threshold.

"Si?"

Christine was cutting the cigar, the guillotine cutter sliced neatly through the cap. "Why is President Sanderson here?"

He sighed, putting his thoughts into order. "Cuba, she has changed a lot. Si? Yet, her soul. That is and will always be the same."

"So I have been told. Is that what this is all about?"

"The battle for Cuba's soul. Si."

Christine snorted. "A battle? During a festival!"

"President Sanderson and El Presidente are waging it right now," Rafael said, turning to leave.

"And who then is leading the resistance?"

As he closed the door, he said simply, "The man who always has. Welcome home, señora."

The heavy door clicked shut, leaving Christine Moore alone in the room. She took a box of matches from next to the humidor then laid out three. Christine took the first, lit it, and then held it near the foot of the cigar. Slowly, she turned the cigar in her fingers, toasting it until the match was burnt down to near her fingertips. She dropped it into an ashtray then quickly grabbed the second, lighting it and once again holding it near the foot of the Habano.

She stared at the flame as it ate away at the wooden match. She felt relaxed; the ritual of cigars always calmed her. The heat licked her finger, bringing her back to reality. The match dropped into the ashtray, the flame dying slowly as Christine took up the last match and repeated the moves, but this time, she put the head of the cigar in her mouth then as she held the flame near the foot once more, she puffed on the cigar. The flame leapt into the air, hitting the cigar.

Christine puffed once, twice, thrice, and then dropped the match. She took the cigar then held it in front of her and blew gently. The foot glowed, completely lit.

"Perfect," she said to herself as she smoked. Her mouth held the cigar as she took the envelope. On the front in neat, pretty handwriting was CHRISTINE.

She frowned slightly at the writing. It seemed familiar. Her fingers opened the flap then slid the paper out. It read:

MEET AT BODEGUITA, SIT AT YOUR OLD TABLE.

Christine looked at the note, then to the cigar. She sighed. Time to work.

CHAPTER FIVE

Havana at night is truly a sight to behold. If during the day the colors are bright and bold, then at night the city truly comes alive. Everyone is out and about. Some are smoking cigars and just enjoying the atmosphere. Others were trying to find that next big party to join in. Music engulfs everyone and the senses are dazzled by the plumes of smoke emerging from nearly everyone and everywhere. The lines to get into clubs, bars, and restaurants are too long to imagine.

This is Havana during the Habanos Festival.

Christine made her way across the borders of New New Havana, into New Havana and then into Old Havana where the buildings were seriously in need of repair. Some were propped up by beams of wood. Others, you could see had collapsed then had been partially cleared with rooms exposed and the people living inside waving happily at the passerbys. Damn, she had missed this place.

Men of all ages approached her; some to ask for a date, they were gringos, others wanted to sell her the "finest Cubans in the world" at a steep discount. She waved all away. Christine moved as if in a trance, her legs doing all the work.

Christine stopped in front of the Castillo de San Salvador de la Punta. She stared out across Havana Bay. The luxury boats were new to her eyes. But the smaller skiffs and dingies reminded her of that old book, the one about the fisherman. She never read it, but everyone told her that it is the quintessential Cuban book, even though it was written by an American.

The stars and the moon twinkled and sparkled in the black water. A breeze swept across the bay and Christine breathed it in deeply. There was something oddly calming about the sea air for her. She loved it. Opening her eyes, Christine spotted spotlights high in the sky above the old Fortaleza de San Carlos de la Cabaña, the fortress that the Spanish built to protect Havana Bay from sea attacks because of the vulnerability of Castillo De Los Tres Reyes Del Morro, an old castle that stands at the heads of Havana Bay.

Christine didn't know if there was an event there or if someone had decided to have a party at La Cabaña, but she would have to check that out. Later.

Turning down Agramonte, she ignored the prostitutes and their pimps. The allure of the flesh would have to wait. Then a turn onto Animas, cutting across Avenida Bélgica, and then finally onto Empedrado, home to La Bodeguita del Medio.

#

La Bodeguita del Medio is THE place in Havana to go for a cigar and the best mojito in the world. That is if you believe the marketing hype. Since 1942, the restaurant-bar has been one of the best tourist destinations in Havana. Pablo Neruda, Josignacio, Gabriel Garcia Marquez, Nat King Cole, and Margaux Hemingway all were regulars of the place at one time or another. The man himself, Ernest Hemingway, was not.

The line stretched along the street, but Christine was able to get to the head by smiling seductively at all the men. It paid to be a woman. The bouncer at the front didn't look too pleased at this floozy making eyes at him.

"¿Estás en la lista, chica," he asked while holding a clipboard at an odd angle.

"Naturalmente, guapo," she answered with a swish of her hair. She touched his face without warning then walked in.

All over the walls are graffiti. This is encouraged by the owners. It makes the place feel lived in and has always been the way. Periodically, they repaint the walls so new notes and quotes can be added. But the one constant is the most famous quote on the wall. In uneven scrawl it reads "My mojito in La Bodeguita, My daiquiri in El Floridita." Under that is the signature of

Hemingway. There is no proof that Papa was ever there, but it makes for a great story and the turistas all take photos of it.

Christine moved through the crowd of people, all trying to get a puro and drink, past the band playing Chan Chan, the most well-known Compay Segundo song then into the back.

Here it was quieter; the music could still be heard but the people in this part of the building were smoking cigars and having private conversations. Most were discussing the talks between the two presidents. A couple were planning to smuggle cigars and other contraband into the USA. A small group were negotiating prices for entry and transport to Miami. *Some things never change*, Christine thought.

Only one table was empty. A sign on it read "Reservado." It was her table, the one where she always conducted meetings and recruitments. Someone had gone out of their way to organize this. La Bodeguita never took reservations. Christine slid into one of the four chairs and waved a waiter over.

"Tomar, señortia?"

"Si, un mojito, por favor. Clasico."

The waiter nodded. Turned. Stopped then looked back. "¿La señora estará deseando un Habano?"

Christine nodded with a smile. She always loved the Cigar Girls that worked for Habanos S.A. in partnership with La Bodeguita.

The waiter nodded again then walked away.

The song swept over her. Chan Chan had always made her melancholy even though the song was about two lovers building a house and that they go to the beach to fetch sand and during this become aroused. For Christine, it was the music itself, the four notes that crawled inside her heart and squeezed it. Perhaps it reminded her of the past or what might happen in the future. Right now, Christine didn't care to find out.

Christine closed her eyes, memories appearing in her mind. As the song continued, tears welled up. She had to shake her head. *Focus*, she told herself.

"¿Que puro, señora?"

Christine's eyes snapped open. She looked up at the young beauty holding a tray lined with various brands and vitolas. Also on it were a cutter, cedar spills, matches, and a butane lighter.

"What do you recommend?"

The Cigar Girl smiled; both were admiring the other. "The Montecristo is always good. But my favourite today is the Bolivar."

Christine nodded her approval.

As the waiter returned with the fabled cocktail, the young lady picked a Bolivar Belicoso Fino from the tray, rolled it between her fingers slightly, took a cutter then snipped the cap. The chunk of tobacco fell to the tray as the lady looked at Christine. "Match, spill, or lighter?"

Christine leaned forward slightly and with a smile said, "You choose, guapa."

With a giggle, she handed the stick to Christine, then picked up the box of matches and one of the cedar spills. The match fizzed and sputtered as she struck it across the box. When it had burnt enough, she used it to light the thin end of the spill. The aroma of the burning wood filled the area. Holding the spill at a forty-five-degree angle, the lady waited.

Christine guided the delicate hands towards her mouth, where the cigar waited. Christine used the lit wood to toast and then light the puro completely. After taking a deep pull, she let the smoke escape her lips slowly. It tasted wonderfully smooth. As she exhaled, her breath blew out the spill, "Muchisimas gracias."

The girl nodded, picked up the tray then sashayed away.

Christine picked up the mojito and stared at the condensation that had formed on the glass.

"Now if that wasn't the sexiest thing I've seen in forever," a silky voice said.

Christine lowered the glass as a ball-achingly gorgeous brunette sat across from her. The woman smiled sweetly at her. "Hola, Christine. Como estas?"

"¡Ir a la chingada, Adriana!"

Adriana Prado laughed as another mojito appeared on the table. She picked it up then took a sip. "Careful, cariña. Those Mexicans will ruin your pretty tongue."

"What my pretty tongue does," Christine said as she took a long draw on the cigar, "is none of your business." She blew the smoke at the Cuban then drained her mojito in one gulp.

Adriana pouted. "That's no way to speak to your contact."

Christine's eyes bulged slightly. "You have got to be fucking kidding?"

The Cuban smiled cheekily with a shake of her head.

"Didn't they tell you?"

"Who?... Station Master or Juan de Dios?"

Adriana nodded as the waiter reappeared with a mojito for Christine.

"I haven't spoken to Juan yet. I thought this was his idea."

"En serio?" Adriana asked as she casually looked around the room. People were now leaving, and the place seemed oppressive; even the music had stopped. "Does this really look like his type of place?"

Christine sipped the drink between puffs on the cigar. "...True." She giggled. "His tastes have always been elsewhere."

Both ladies laughed loudly. The bar staff looked at them curiously.

"Why are you here?" Christine held up her hand, stopping Adriana from speaking. "I know WHY you are here. But...you should be dead!"

The Cuban held up her hands. "What can I say? Juan knows a good asset when he sees one."

"Asset? Is that what they call you now? I remember what he used to call you."

Adriana tilted her head to the side slightly, curiosity getting to her.

"A worthless cunt!"

Christine got to her feet, knocking the table and nearly spilling the tasty beverages. "Tell them that I am not going to be partnered with a lying, deceitful whore. I'll do this with him, or by myself."

Adriana watched as Christine grabbed her drink and finished it. "Sit down, Christine," she said with such authority that it made the other woman stop. "Sit down. Now," she repeated.

"Why should I?"

The Cuban sighed. "Fine. Don't. Go back to the Nacional and contact Station Master. See what happens. But, before you do, you should know what is at stake."

The smoke billowed from the foot of the cigar, clinging to Christine, surrounding her in a halo. "Save the world. I suppose."

"Apart from the fine print. Si."

Christine sat, sullenly back in her chair. "And what, pray tell, is the fine print?"

Adriana held her glass to her mouth, taking a long sip before she answered, "Prevent not one, but two presidential assassinations then stop a man more dangerous than any terrorist. A man worse than Harry Lime and Richard Roper put together."

The words hung in the air the same way that the smoke did. Christine stared at Adriana. "That is high praise indeed, coming from you."

"Isn't history grand," Adriana said with a chuckle.

Christine's answer was to get up then walk out the back.

#

The alley behind La Bodeguita was uninviting. But for Christine, anywhere was better than with that woman. She leaned against the wall staring at the night sky. She sighed and stared at the glowing foot of her cigar. It pulsed slightly as a breeze swept through the alley.

A clang startled her ever so slightly and Christine spun to face it. Her arms up instantly ready for an attack.

"¿Puedes ayudarme, señorita?" a gruff slightly slurred voice begged from the darkness. Christine had to squint slightly, trying to spot the owner of the voice.

"No."

"¿Puedes ayudarme, señorita?" the voice said again as another clang sounded. Slowly from a pile of trash a tall, skeletal hobo emerged. He was wearing rags that left very little to the imagination. "Puedes ayudarme," he bellowed.

Christine shook her head, her eyes spotting the oozing pustules on the exposed skin. *Sick,* she thought as she slowly started to move away.

The hobo began to shamble forward, arms outstretched reaching for her. His eyes were devoid of rationality. Drool hung from his lips.

Her feet spread in a ready stance. Christine had the feeling that this man, if he was still one, was going to try something. The hand holding the cigar readied itself, to drive it into one of the sockets.

"I understand if you don't want to do this. Our history isn't the…cleanest," Adriana said as she exited the building. She stopped dead in her tracks and stared at the almost naked man. "Having fun without me?"

"Shut up."

The man turned his head at the sound of Adriana's voice. "Puedes ayudarme."

Adriana laughed. "Not on your life, cariño."

A slight tilt of the head and the man tried to reason what was said. After a moment, he snarled and raised both arms. "Watch it," Adriana warned. She needn't have done so.

The hobo lunged for Christine who spun and drove the cigar into the dead eye socket. The eyeball exploded from the heat and force. Clear liquid spurted at Christine, followed by blood. Christine ducked and spun around the man who growled and then followed her.

Her leg caught on his leg and she tripped.

Seconds later, the man as on top of her, snarling, drooling, and trying to sink his teeth into her soft supple flesh. Christine fought with all her might but for a man with very little muscle mass, he was surprisingly strong. "Help me!"

Adriana shook her head as she leant against the wall. "You look fine."

Christine slammed her knee into the man's stomach. There was a sickening crunch which was followed by a tearing sound; the skin broke and stomach, intestines, and slime unraveled all over her legs.

Forcing herself not to vomit, Christine tried head-butting. Three times her forehead collided with the hobo's nose. Each smack was followed by the tell-tale sound of bone splintering, then cracking and finally a mushy squelching sound as the bone found its way up and into the brain.

There was a slight groan from the hobo then he went rigid and collapsed, rolling off of her. Christine slowly sat up and looked in disgust at the mess that covered her and was flowing out of the dead body. "What the fuck?"

Adriana walked over to her and helped her up, making sure, naturally, not to get any of the entrails on her. "There, told you you had it covered."

"Covered!" Christine spun to glare at the Cuban. "You could have helped me, you selfish bitch! And for your information, our history is as far from clean as possible. Hitler has cleaner history than what happened!"

"All Cubans should shoot," Adriana said, "and shoot good." The Cuban took two steps, grabbing Christine's arms then spun her, their bodies intertwining, connecting.

"No," Christine exhaled with a swift kick to Adriana's groin.

Adriana dropped to the ground, gasping and holding her crotch. She looked up as Christine vanished into the night.

CHAPTER SIX

"Fuck me," Christine exclaimed after locking the door behind her. Her breathing had started to slow, but her heartbeat was rapid. Picking up a linen napkin, she wiped the sweat from her brow. The run back to the Nacional had drained her. She then quickly changed her clothes; the blood and sweat and acid fluids had dried and began to reek.

After getting a Cuba Libre ready, more Cuban rum than libre, and a cigar lit up, Christine went to the open balcony. The outside air was cool on her face, the sea breeze rejuvenating. A long sigh escaped her and Christine was at ease. A street band was playing and the soothing notes of the guitar washed over the room.

Turning, Christine made her way over to the small bar area she had created. As she did, the Cuba Libre disappeared into her. It didn't take long for the next one to follow its friend. Christine started making a third then decided to sip it. She couldn't be hungover during the operation. That's what she told herself anyway. As the coke filled the class and condensation formed on the outside, her eyes darted across the table. Rum, limes, coke, cigars, a satellite phone...

Wait! A phone? That wasn't there earlier. She placed the glass on the table, and then picking up a stirrer, she gently nudged the phone. It slid across the table slightly, but nothing more. Christine waited a moment then she flipped the device. It clattered to the floor. And there it lay.

Christine knelt down and quickly grabbed the phone. Going through the contacts, there was only one. The name was S. She sighed as she pressed dial. This was not going to be pretty.

"Report," the curt old voice answered after the first ring.

"It's nice to hear your voice too, Station Master," Christine said cheerfully as she sipped on the refreshing beverage. "How's tricks? The famil—"

"—Report!" the voice said, making her stop.

"Well," she began, "the flight was quite wonderful. Thank you for the private jet. Cuba has changed a whole lot. And oh, yeah, fucking Adriana is the damn contact!" her voice echoed in the room. The waves kept crashing against the sea wall and the music continued.

It seemed like forever, the silence, then finally, "And?"

Christine laughed; that was the last thing she expected. "And?" she repeated. "And that cunt snake is the person I'm supposed to be working with here? Don't you remember what she did to us! To me!"

"Enough," Station Master said, sounding tired. "I've made a grave mistake sending you. Pack your bags. Get back to the Station House. Now."

"Station Master!" Christine began. "You sent me here because you know I can do the job. Havana was mine for five years. Adriana Prado was an unexpected surprise."

"I had not noticed," Station Master's sardonic voice echoed in Christine's mind. "Do your job, Christine. Return a hero and all will be forgiven."

Christine paced the main area of the suite. "I will. I can. Just...why didn't you give me all the intel?"

A long pause from her boss. Then, "If I had. Would you still have gone?" Christine said nothing. She stared out the window, at the darkness. "I thought so." Station Master continued, "Your level is need to know and this was a piece of information that you did not need to know." Christine opened her mouth to speak, but his voice stopped her. "If you have such a problem, why not go straight to the head of Cuban Intelligence? What's his name? That man with the limp and horrible taste in clothes."

"Juan de Dios," Christine answered while suppressing a smile.

"Yes. That's the one. Never could stand him..." Station Master paused, lost in a thought. "Get him to replace the woman, if it's too unbearable. Now," he cleared his throat, "Report."

Christine straightened slightly, her training taking over. "The festival has been happening for one day now. Everyone I have spoken to so far has given me nothing. Apparently tomorrow, President Sanderson is paying a visit to Pinar del Rio. Intel says that there might be an attempt on him. Other than that, nothing else has come up." She drained the Cuba Libre in her hand. Suddenly, she was exhausted.

"Have you confirmed this?"

Christine gulped, her throat all of a sudden dry. "Not as yet, sir."

"Then confirm it before acting. What about Jeremiah Banks?"

"Only whispers in the dark that he is returning to free Cuba from the USA."

The silence from the other end of the phone was suffocating. The seconds ticked over and Christine was starting to get worried.

"Anything else?" Station Master finally asked.

Christine thought. She wasn't sure if she should tell him about the dying and the attack. *Maybe*, she mused, *it's all connected. Better report everything.*

"Yes, Station Master. When I was on my way to the hotel, I noticed that there are many people her sick. And," she continued before he could cut in, "before you say anything, I know there are sick. But I'm talking about people standing on the streets looking dead. I saw a boy, a child, get dragged to the ground by a dog. There was no sound! He didn't scream or anything. If I didn't know any better, I'd say that he was already dead and his body hadn't caught up." She took a breath before continuing. "Then tonight, I met her and, well, a man tried to attack me."

"You must expect that in a place like Havana."

"Yes, sir. But the odd thing was that he didn't try to rape me. He wanted to eat me. As if I was a slab of meat. He could barely speak and think... Almost like a zomb—"

"Continue the mission," Station Master said, stopping her in mid-sentence. "Keep an ear about Jeremiah Banks."

"Yes Station—" Christine started but he had already hung up. She looked at the phone then at her surroundings. "Nice talking to you too."

The lights flared up then everything blinked into darkness.

\#

"Damn it," Christine said as she stumbled around the room. Her arms were outstretched, waving blindly as each step taken was a nail-biter.

Christine had forgotten about the rolling black-outs that happened across Havana. It made living here fun if you weren't used to it. Her feet shuffled across the carpeted floor. *Now I know how the blind feel*, she thought to herself.

Finally, she made it to the window; it was closed and the shades drawn tight. Christine made short work of the tie and the curtains fell open, letting moonlight spill into the room, bathing everything in its glow. The eeriness was beautiful. Christine smiled. Station Master was right. She needed to speak with Juan, that old caballero. But first thing's first. A shower.

The water was warm, but it kept sputtering and blasting her firstly with hot water then with cold. Christine laughed. She had indeed missed the Cuban lifestyle.

As the water cleansed her, washing away the grime from so many years away, her mind started to clear too. And as it did, a thought formed. Why didn't Juan contact her directly for a sit-down? *After all*, she thought, *they had been through so much when she was first stationed here*. He must have had his reasons. But what could they have been? Christine shook her head. More thoughts were creeping in, ones that she did not need at this moment. Maybe later.

Logic. That's what was needed right now. Christine started to make a list. A very special list.

1) Speak to Juan and get all the intel needed.

2) If everything is golden, then she would go to Pinar del Rio and work with Adriana.

3) The first real sign of Jeremiah Banks, and Christine Moore would kill him.

Christine smiled at that thought as the hotel light's flickered back on. *Lovely*, she thought as she climbed out of the shower and started drying herself with a towel.

She had wrapped it around her hair. Christine had never been one for modesty. Then she went back into the main room, took a swig from the open bottle of rum, and picked up the phone.

"Hola," she said when the other end was answered. "I was wondering if I could speak with Rafael? He must still be here."

"Uno momento," the voice at the other end said curtly.

"Hola, this is Rafael," the voice was tired.

"Why don't you go home?" Christine said.

"I am, dear señorita," the manager said with a laugh. "What can I do for you?"

"Juan de Dios. I need to see him."

"Señora… Christine… I just can't ring and demand."

"Oh yes you can, Rafael," she said. "You just tell him that it's me."

"Are you sure?"

"Yes. Call him. Then let me know where we are meeting."

She could hear Rafael breathing, calculating the risks of ringing the head of Cuban Intelligence at this time of night. If he said no, then she would have to take matters into her own hands. Yes? Then Christine Moore would have a fighting chance.

"Si, señora. Allow me a moment."

Christine fist-pumped the air in victory. "I wait with baited breath."

CHAPTER SEVEN

The Buena Vista Social Club was THE place to be in the 1940s. If you were a musician or just enjoyed the best son, boleros, or rumbas in all of the Caribbean then this was it. Some of the greatest Cuban musicians played there before it was closed in the late 1940s. On any night, one could go and see Compay Segundo, Ibrahim Ferrer, or even Rubén González hanging out, jamming with new and old songs, all the while drinking, smoking, and laughing. It was truly a special time.

Then it all ended and these greats and many more disappeared into obscurity. That was until the 1990s when an American found them and created a new band named after the fabled place. It brought Cuban music to the limelight and created opportunities for all the old guard. The band continued to tour even with the members passing on. The Buena Vista Social Club Orchestra, as it was now known, would just replace them. Then in 2015, the band decided that was it. No more touring. And the world music scene cried.

Now, in Havana there opened a new place, The Buena Vista Social Club. Almost as popular as La Bodeguita and La Floridita. The New Buena Vista is not exactly a speakeasy, nor is it a hole-in-the-wall. Mixing the history of Cuban Music with all the trappings of a modern establishment, all walks of life venture into the building, which was where Christine found herself, standing in front of the plain building. No signs advertising where she was or what was inside. Not even a bouncer.

The instructions had been clear. Rafael had called her and

said, "It's done, Christine. The Buena Vista Social Club. Go to the door. Knock and wait."

"The Buena Vista? That doesn't exist," she replied.

"A car is out front that will take you."

"Wait. Rafael, where is it? What is it?"

He had hung up the phone.

The driver had said nothing and had taken many twists and turns on the way. He opened the door for her eventually when they stopped. Then just as quickly drove away into the night, leaving her feeling bamboozled.

One loud sharp bang on the door with her fist echoed down the street, most likely inside too. Instinctively, Christine cracked her knuckles, stretched her back and neck, loosening up for anything, unexpected.

The door opened and the classic song "El Cuarto de Tula" washed over her. The air was thick with cigar smoke and the sounds of people laughing and not having a care in the world. Christine stepped across the threshold.

#

Inside was magical. Christine looked around at all the people. All were dressed for a wonderful evening out. Linen suits, panama hats, the occasional fedora, and the ladies a mixture of dresses, skirts, and pants. Not one of them was a hipster or turista. It made her smile at the sights, smells, and sounds. Her eyes went to the stage where a small five-piece band were belting out the song.

It was one of the best classic Cuban songs to dance to. The lyrics were simple and easy. They talked about a woman whose house had caught fire and that each member of the band was mentioned as having helped. And though the lyrics were simple and free-form, the rhythm was irresistible. Try as she might, Christine could not help but shake her hips and move to the music. She laughed and smiled, enjoying herself properly since arriving in Havana.

She nodded at them and the singer winked at her cheekily. Christine continued glancing at people dancing, talking, and flirting, trying to find the old distinguished head of Cuban Intelligence. Nada. Amongst the crowd was not any man who resembled him. Christine cursed herself then headed for the bar.

"Un mojito, por favor," she ordered when the bartender spotted her.

"Lo siento, Chica, pero no mojito. Solo Cuba Libre," he said apologetically.

Christine shook her head. "When in Rome."

The bartender nodded as he took a rocks glass. "Make it a highball." Again, the young man nodded as he scooped some ice into the tall glass, followed by a healthy pour of Havana Club Especial. Add some lime juice. Then to top it off, Coca-Cola. A vigorous stirring and voila, a Cuba Libre. He slid it to Christine, followed by a precut Trinidad. She looked at it.

"Compliments of the owner," he said with a big smile.

Christine took the drink, the cigar, and a small lighter. The barman pointed with his head. Christine followed and saw a small empty booth.

Sitting down, Christine began to light the stogie. It was aged perfectly and the flavors were sublime. Whoever owns the place definitely knew how to keep cigars properly. She took a long slow draw on it and savored each of the tastes. Next, she took a sip of the cocktail. Christine had never liked the drink. But now, after so many years away from Cuba, it tasted like ambrosia. She closed her eyes and just drifted, carried away by the music, beverage, and smoke.

"I do hope you're enjoying yourself," an older voice with just the slightest tinge of an accent said.

Christine's eyes snapped open and she grinned despite herself.

Juan de Dios had aged, but he carried himself with a tranquility and grace seen in a much younger man. He, as Christine remembered, was still dressed immaculately. Perfectly pressed linen, a neatly trimmed goatee, white hair slicked back, and that tell-tale twinkle of the eyes that all spy masters have, that love for keeping secrets. In one hand, he held a cane, bamboo and tobacco leaf. The other held a panama hat.

"How's the leg?"

"It hurts sometimes," he said as they sat in the booth. "Only when it is cold. So, luckily never." He laughed as the bartender brought him a daiquiri.

"This is truly a wonderful place," she commented as they

drank.

Juan nodded his thanks as the band finished the song. They took the applause with due modesty then started playing an original piece. His eyes looked at the cigar in her hand. "Do you still like them?"

Christine smiled. "You know me too well, Juan. How long have you had…?" she gestured at the surroundings.

"Long enough to regret not having it earlier," the man said with a slight sorrowful smile. He sipped at his cocktail then furrowed his brow. "Christine, why are you here?"

She blinked. Out of all the questions, that was the one she was not, nor could ever have been, prepared for. "Station Master sent me. The Festival? The presidents?"

"Ah," he nodded, "the old man did say he was going to send someone." He shook his head slightly, dislodging strands of hair. "I would have thought he'd send someone else." His hand moved of its own accord to fix the hair. "You must have done something really impressive to get back into his good graces."

Christine was smiling, though it was forced, as her mind screamed at her to get out of the country. But she couldn't. So she didn't. Instead, "I need information."

"That could have been arranged through Rafael." Juan de Dios waved his hand, like shooing smoke away from his face. "What do you really want?"

"I told you. Information. Everything about the festival this year. Why President Sanderson is really here? Are the rumors true?"

"Rumors?" the old spy master chuckled. "My dear señora. All I have are rumors. Which one are you interested in? The one about President Sanderson trying to beat Clinton's record for interns? Or, how about the Mexicans trying to buy land here? No?" He frowned slightly, his mind racing. Christine new how to play this: keep silent and let the man do all the work. She didn't have to wait long. "Ah!" Juan said with a snap of the fingers. "I know! The rumors about what lies under Guantanamo Bay."

"Juan," she said with fake sorrow, "you know me to well. Please."

"Well," he began, after smiling at all in the room smugly, "the gringos have owned the Bay for years, bought originally to have a base in the Caribbean. Not good enough to have Puerto Rico, eh?"

"Spill it, old man."

"Forgive me, por favor. What happened was that for a brief time during the Cold War, the Russians did something incredibly smart. Or stupid. Depending on who you ask."

Christine had heard this before. Just before she had been exiled by Station Master, a drunkard at La Bodeguita had told her, trying to impress her. She didn't have time for this. "The nuclear base under the Bay? Really Juan? That's the big rumor you have?"

The old man looked cut by her tone of voice. "It's my personal favorite. And, I must say, I tell it exceedingly well." He slumped into the cushioned seat and drank sullenly.

"I'm sorry, dear friend," Christine said. "I'm behind everything here. A day late and talks of an assassination attempt. Your contact has set up an operation but... I don't trust her."

"Her?"

Christine nodded. Juan looked concerned. "I don't know of any operation. But," here he laughed harshly, "there is much I no longer know."

"What? Aren't you the head of CI?"

"My abuela had a saying," he said. "Just because you are the head, doesn't mean you have the brain. There is much they don't tell me. Bureaucracy at its finest."

"Damn. I need to know one thing. Just tell me one thing, Juan."

"If I can."

"Is Jeremiah Banks back?"

CHAPTER EIGHT

Christine didn't wait for the old man to finish talking. The moment she had mentioned Jeremiah Banks' name, Juan forgot how to speak in any language. Five minutes of him babbling on about how he acquired the new Buena Vista was all she could take. "Excuse me," she had said curtly, stood up then left without another word.

She found herself wondering the streets. The cigar still lit, hung loosely from her lips. Getting a glimpse of herself in a window made her feel stupid. Her hand went up and removed the cigar. Her feet kept moving of their own accord, turning here and there.

Christine told herself the most important survival rule for being in Havana: if you get lost, just walk towards the sound of the sea. From the Malecón, it's easy to get where you want to go, which was where she seemed to be heading towards as the crashing of waves grew louder and louder.

Rough hands grabbed her, two pairs, and she was dragged into an alley. Christine didn't scream. There was no need to. Her training was rusty, but men are easy to take down, especially drunk beasts.

"Yum yum!" the one with the lazy-eye said as he licked his lips. They had thrown Christine against the wall and had surrounded her. There were four of them. Lazy-eye was the ring leader. The bald one had a large machete in his hand and was flicking the blade with his thumb. The third one looked normal, just a rapist in training. The last one was big. He had had training at some point.

"Why don't you go with one of your boyfriends here?" Christine said as she took a long draw on the cigar.

Lazy-eye took a step closer to her. "Careful, my sweet. You wouldn't want to lose that perfect tongue... Just yet." He laughed then looked at his friends. They all laughed except for Mr. Training. He leaned against the other wall with his arms crossed, looking completely unimpressed.

"Run away, little maricas," she said with a wave of her hand. "I'm too busy and you all need a bath."

"I'll have a bath, with your tongue," Baldy said with a sneer as he reached out to her.

"Don't kill her," Lazy-eye said. "Just have some fun."

"Honey," Christine said without a care, "you wouldn't know fun. Except for goats and pigs."

"Bring me her tongue!"

Baldy was the first to lunge at her. Christine spun on her foot, whipping the other into the air. The Cuban ducked but as he came up, he got a cigar in the eye for his trouble. He screamed, clutching at the stub that was lodged in his socket. Blood seeped out and down his face. Christine slammed her foot into his chest, sending him backwards into Normal. They both collapsed.

The machete came down hard and fast. Luckily, Christine saw the glint of the blade and side-stepped it casually. The blade whistled past her, grazing her left arm. Christine cursed then with two moves had the machete in her hands. She kicked Lazy-eye in the crotch then as he sank to his knees, the machete found itself buried into his head. His good eye hung from its socket as blood squirted high into the air and splattered the wall.

Christine flinched and groaned as Normal landed a one-two punch on her kidneys. His hands gripped her shoulders and as he spun her, he launched her into the air. Christine collided with the wall. Her face bled as she slid down the rough surface. The wind was knocked from her and she clawed to get to her feet.

Baldy was upon her now, kicking her in the chest and sides. Christine lashed out as best she could, but her blows landed on the ground.

Normal and Baldy stood over her, laughing as she coughed blood. "Let's have some real fun," Normal said as his hands started at his belt.

"No," Mr. Training said finally. He hadn't moved from his spot at all.

"¿Que?" Baldy said. He fidgeted with the cigar but whimpered and dropped his hand.

"You heard me. Beat her all you want. But. Do. Not. Fuck. Her." The big man took a step towards the other two men. Normal was eyeballing the machete.

"Why not?" he asked with a sneer.

"Orders are orders."

"Fuck orders," Normal said as he dived for the blade.

As he landed, his face froze in surprise as Christine swiped at his neck. She had crawled over during the small discussion then had waited. The rusty knife got stuck in the artery and Normal clutched and gurgled as the life faded from his eyes.

She rolled onto her back, breathing heavily then looked at Mr. Training who had Baldy in a headlock and was swinging him around, crashing the thug into the walls, trash cans, and mounds of garbage. Then the man spun quickly, let go, and watched as Baldy came to a stop in a pile of garbage. The sound of glass shattering and shredding clothes made the big thug laugh. Christine watched as he went over to the pile, reached in, felt around then pulled up Baldy. He was cut and bruised but still ready for a fight.

"Go fuck your mother," he spat.

"Already did. Lousy lay," Mr. Training said and with a casual movement, he snapped Baldy's neck. The vertebrae popped out at a hideous angle.

"Fucking amateurs," Mr. Training said to himself as the limp body crumpled to the ground. He wiped his hands on the dirt clothes, making sure there was no trace of blood. Then he stood and looked around. He sighed, happy.

Christine started to crawl away, hoping to find a weapon, but at each movement, she groaned loudly. The noise brought Mr. Training back to the situation. He walked over to her.

"Forgive the poor attitude of my compatriots," he said casually. "My, my, my," he continued, "you don't look so good.

We must get you to a doctor, post haste!"

Christine tried to kick at him but as he bent down, she lost consciousness.

#

Christine's eyes fluttered open. She moaned slightly, her arm moving up to her face instinctively. Halfway up, it stopped. Her eyes focused on the restraint wrapped around her right arm. She slowly turned her head, fighting fear, and looked at her left arm. There it was in its own restraint and a bandage wrapped tightly around her wound.

"Oh good," said a sardonic voice, "you're awake."

The voice belonged to a young man. A doctor most likely, Christine thought. But, where was she?

"You're somewhere safe," the doctor continued. "Lucky someone found you in that alley. You had lost quite a lot of blood. Not to mention your wounds and what you did to those men. How did you pop a vertebrae out of the neck? I mean, I've seen some gruesome accidents in my time. But that?" He whistled. "The restraints? Well, those were for my protection. They brought you in and the moment I started to work on you, you tried to bite my face. Kicking and punching anything you could. So, I had to give you a small sedative to make my life easier. And do I get a thank you for all my hard work? Not even a peso. And there's the chance that the police will be coming a-knocking on my door in the next day or so. I don't know what's happening to the world." He took a sip of water from a bottle. "Don't try to talk. I had to bandage your face and jaw. Nothing permanent but better safe than sorry. Scars? No need to worry. All the cuts and grazes are superficial. Keep in bed for the next day or two and you'll be right as rain." Another sip and he started for the door. Christine moaned after him.

"Sorry?" he said, turning back. "Only five hours. It's almost eight in the morning. Well. Good luck."

And with that, Christine was left alone. She laid her head back onto the pillow and closed her eyes. Ignoring the pain, she focused on what happened after the fight. Mr. Training had said something about apologies and that it was necessary to send a message. Christine had rolled over onto her back, so as to see what was happening. But the man had covered her eyes as he said... *Damn,*

Christine thought. She couldn't hear him for the blood filling her ears. Only two words had stuck in her mind: WMDs and the Bay.

As the door clicked open, so did her eyes. She couldn't move to see who had entered the room but the footsteps were light. Not heavy like a man's. The air was filled with perfume. Lavender. *Fuck me*, Christine thought. It had to be Adriana.

"What did you do?" Adriana said as she stared, jaw open at Christine.

All Christine could do was mumble a response and try to wave her hands.

"Never mind," Adriana said as she sat next to the bed. "Listen. You were found surrounded by dead men. That must've been one hell of a fight. Do you remember anything? Oh, my sweet, what did they do to your face?" She reached out and slowly undid the bandages.

The blood-stained dressings fell to the floor and Christine flexed her jaw. "Who…who found me?"

"Some drunk looking for a place to piss," Adriana replied as she studied the grazed face. "He called Juan who called me. You're back at the Nacional. Don't worry. Everything is going to be okay." She spoke gently, like one does to a dangerous animal. "In a couple of hours, I'll contact The Station and you'll be back home getting the proper care."

"No fucking way," Christine said, struggling with her bonds. "There's more at stake here than just the gringo president's life…will you help me!"

Adriana undid the restraints and watched as Christine rubbed her wrists. "What do you mean?"

Christine stood up and walked into the main room and straight over to the bar. She poured herself a tall rum then drank deeply from it. "One of the attackers said something just before I passed out. I think it's a long shot but you never know." She took another drink as Adriana watched from the doorway.

"Go on."

"Guantanamo. There are WMDs there."

"Puta madre!"

Christine nodded her head. "You know what this means? Jeremiah Banks isn't going to kill Sanderson. He's going to kidnap him and use him to get the launch codes." She finished her drink then went over to the balcony. Her eyes gazed at the sun. A deep sigh escaped her.

"Wait. Aren't they supposed to be Russian?" Adriana said as she wrapped her arms around Christine's waist.

"The story goes," she said as she removed the arms from around her body, "that after the Missile Crisis, the Russians sold the codes to the gringos; make some cash and use it as a show of good faith. Why do you think that base is so state-of-the-art?"

Adriana stepped aside as Christine went for another drink. "You've got a plan. Right?"

Christine smiled slightly. "Yep. Today is the Pinar del Rio tour, yeah? So one of us should be there in case an attack happens. It should be you. You and Juan can coordinate the area better than I. While you do that, I'll pay a visit to the Bay. I can pose as a citizen looking for asylum and have a lookie-look."

As she drank, Adriana shook her head.

"What?"

"I've got a contact at the Bay. It'll be easier for me to get in."

"How...you...what?"

Adriana smiled. "When you got it, flaunt it."

"I remember," Christine said as she finished her third drink. "So, while you have fun playing Nancy Drew, I'll be tip-toeing through the tulips?"

"I never understood those idioms. But, yes. I'll let Juan know to expect you so he can alert his men."

Christine went over to the door, opened it, and waited. "Go on. It's a long drive to the Bay."

Adriana followed her and stood on the threshold. "How about a kiss for luck?"

The door gave her a gentle kiss as it closed.

CHAPTER NINE

Christine's body ached and her face was sore, but the graze was not noticeable. She hadn't slept much, tossing and turning, trying to get the image of Adriana naked and wanting her out of her mind. Rum helped with that. Before the sun rose, she had gotten out of bed, examined herself thoroughly and, happy with the results, showered, dressed then left for Pinar del Rio.

The two-hour bus ride hadn't been completely unpleasant. Christine had talked her way onto one of the buses, found a seat next to a skinny old reporter then waited. The reporter didn't say a word to her. He was busy writing in a little notebook. Christine casually glanced at the scribbling.

"You writing about cigars?"

"No," the man was blunt and his manner said it all. Leave me alone.

"Really? I love cigars, don'cha know," she said, doing her best Katherine Hepburn impression. The reporter didn't look up. "Always have. Daddy got me into it. Wanted a son, instead got me! I had to learn to smoke them otherwise Daddy wouldn't have paid me any attention, don'cha know." She elbowed the older man conspiratorially.

He closed the notebook, fixed his glasses then looked at her. "What do you want?"

The bus roared to life and started the one hundred and eighty-eight-kilometer journey. The other passengers talked loudly, singing songs, drinking rums and cokes while enjoying cigars. Christine tried to look shocked at such a question. "I was only curious. No need to jump down my throat. It's a long trip and I thought you might enjoy some…stimulating conversation." She pouted then looked out the window.

The reporter sighed, adjusting his glasses. "I'm sorry, miss. It's a dull flight here and, well, I hate cigars."

Christine turned. "Really? Then why," she drew out the syllable, sounding like Blanche in Streetcar, "why are you here? Didn't anyone tell you that there is a cigar festival happening?"

The older man couldn't help but laugh. "Yes, but, I'm here for the political agenda."

"Political? Cigars aren't political."

"They can be," he said. "Why else would the United States president come here?"

"Hmmmmm, for the cigars!"

"Maybe. Maybe not." He opened the notebook and started scribbling in it. Christine looked; he wasn't writing in words but in symbols. Short-hand. *Clever boy*, she thought to herself.

"Well, maybe he is but, I can tell you something," she said, her tone changing to that of a person with authority over everyone. "He isn't here because of Guantanamo."

That did the trick!

"Really? Why would you say that? The president is allowed to pay a visit."

Christine laughed and gently caressed the hand. Her eyes skimmed the page.

Sanderson won't make any deals where terrorists could make a base on Cuba.

False, she thought.

Cuba needs to be a territory. Russia won't help them at all.

Boring.

If there are WMDs at Guantanamo, then Sanderson would be here to bargain for their return.

Maybe.

Jeremiah Banks?

"Oh honey," she said quietly. "I've lived here for years and not once has a president visited. It's just not done. Why would he do it now?"

The older reporter looked at her, his eyes slightly misty; from age or drink, Christine couldn't tell. He licked his lips, trying to make a decision.

"Think about it," Christine continued, "The only reason for the president to come to Cuba would be for...maybe one of three things." She held up her hand, counting fingers one by one. "First, to negotiate the end of the embargo and Cuba becoming another territory. I don't think so, don'cha know. Second, maybe there is something important at Guantanamo that he needs, or has to check on personally. What it could be, I don't know. And last...well...he could be after a criminal."

"Jeremiah Banks!" the reporter said without thinking. He clamped his mouth shut, turning bright red with embarrassment. Christine nodded her head.

"Maybe, honey. But he's a ghost. Right? A whispered name in the Caribbean to scare people."

The older man shook his head vigorously. "He isn't! He's real! I know he is! That's why I'm here."

"Oh?" Christine feigned surprise. Hopefully, this guy could give her some proper information. *Worst thing would be he's a crackpot*, she thought.

"Yes! I've been tracking Jeremiah Banks for fifteen years. I'm positive that's why President Sanderson is here: to discuss the extradition of a war criminal. See, when Banks first arrived in Cuba, he had nothing. Imagine Humphrey Bogart in Casablanca. He started to invest in businesses all over the island, starting in Santiago then moving into the mountains and coming to his Holy Land. Havana. From here, he was able to buy the police, the port, officials... You name it, he had a hand in it. All the while he started importing things people needed. See, Cuba has a thriving black-market and Banks wanted to be top dog. So he started with small things. Toys for children. Then some clothes. Bed linens and on and on until he got into medicine."

"That doesn't make sense. Cuba has the best free health care in the world."

"True. But there are certain medications that are hard to come by. That's what Jeremiah Banks specialized in... He built up an empire that eventually controlled the entirety of the Cuban black-market. Then shortly after President Felipe Esposito was elected, he just disappeared. No word. No sightings. Nothing at all. That's why I'm here. If the presidents are going to talk, then Banks will make sure it goes wrong."

They sat in silence as the bus exited Havana. The countryside was beautiful, greens as far as the eye could see. The highway didn't go by the coast, which annoyed Christine, but not nearly as much as this crazy person. *Reporter indeed*, she thought. *Fuck my life sideways.*

"How do you know all this?" she asked.

"Research. My life's work is on him."

Christine nodded her head, thinking of an excuse to change seats.

"I got word from a contact living in Cuba that there had been sightings. He's back."

"Oh, really?" Christine said, her heart sinking as she realized that the scribblings were not short-hand but in fact a made-up language. "And how do you know this 'contact'?"

He smiled with pride. "Reddit."

#

Christine had hastily swapped seats. She was now sitting next to a bear of a man who was deeply asleep, a panama hat pulled down over his head. *Good idea*, she thought and positioned herself for a nap.

The bus hit a large pothole that made everyone jump, startled awake, except for Christine. Her eyes opened slowly, calmly. She looked around. The bus was making its way up a steep incline. There was no road, just dirt, rocks, and large bumps. All around were trees. Palms. Ferns. Tropical. Some would call it paradise. Christine called it the Heartland of Cigars.

Pinar del Rio is where nearly all of the tobacco is grown and used for cigars in Cuba. Sure there are others, but none are as important as Pinar. For within this province lie four areas. Ranches, plantations, whatever you want to call them that sport the perfect soil conditions to grow Tabaco Negro Cubano. Vuelta Abajo is THE land that is the key source of tobacco for the cigars. Here, they grow all types of tobacco that go into the making of a cigar: the wrapper (which covers the cigar), binder (the leaf that gives the cigar its shape), and the filler (where most of the flavors come from). Then there is San Luis, the epicenter for the vegueros (farmers) and where the leaves are used in the Cohiba brand. After that, there is San Juan y Martinez and Semi Vuelta.

Vuelta Abajo is where the tour of Pinar del Rio started and as Christine thought, would be where an attempt on President Sanderson's life would happen. She hoped that Adriana had talked to Juan and everything was organized. She hoped. The reason they have the Habanos Festival in February is because this is the time that the tobacco plants are almost ready for harvesting. Standing at almost 305 centimeters, they are impressive. The crowd in the bus all took photos of the fields and the farmers, making sure each plant was ready for the harvest and that there were no tobacco beetles on the precious leaves. Christine smiled. She loved the sight.

The bus came to a stop and everyone clambered out. There were more buses and more turistas, a mixture of reporters, cameramen, cigar enthusiasts, and the locals who had turned out to catch a glimpse of the President. Among the crowd were men wearing guayaberas, the traditional shirt with four pockets on the front. These were the tour guides and all were trying to get the attention of the turistas. Some were already forming lines, ready to take them around the plantations.

"Disculpe, señorita," an ancient voice said as the equally aged finger tapped her shoulder. Christine spun. The veguero was tiny and had been alive for far too long. He smiled up at her and his face looked as if it was about to split along the wrinkles.

"Si?"

"This is for you." He held up a petite corona-sized cigar. It was band-less. But looked delicious.

"Oh no," Christine said, "I couldn't, but thank you."

The old man shook his head. "This is your cigar, señora. And so is this." In his other hand was a small folded piece of paper.

"Gracias," she said, taking both. The veguero bowed his head slightly then shuffled away.

Christine quickly unfolded the note.

Chris, do us all a favor and stay out of trouble.

CI has this covered.
Love, Ad

"No fucking way," she said to herself as she used her lighter to burn the paper. The ashes floated away while she cut the head off the cigar and got it lit. The flavors were earthy and Christine had found a new favorite.

To all eyes, she looked just like a turista; a gorgeous woman enjoying cigars, the scenery, and life in general. She ignored the tour guides cat-calling at her, trying to get her to join their line. Instead, Christine's eyes were constantly darting around, scanning the crowd for anyone who looked suspicious.

She started to frown. Was this a waste of time?

Had Adriana sent her here so that she wouldn't find out the truth at the Bay?

Wouldn't be the first time, she thought. Her mind started to wander to the past. Christine shook her head. *Not now*, she commanded herself; stay focused on the mission. A quick glance at her watch showed that at any moment President Sanderson would be arriving. But how?

As if on cue, the vegetation began to sway. The dust and earth was kicked up as a powerful man-made wind shot through the area. All eyes went up as panama hats and fedoras were scattered to the four corners.

A small helicopter had appeared in the sky and was circling, looking for a place to land. The pilot must have found it for the vehicle started descending towards them. The turistas, reporters, and vegueros ran, creating a perimeter for the helicopter.

The closer it got, the more violent the wind became. Christine had to shield her eyes and hold the cigar so that she could still see and the cigar would not be wasted.

As soon as the helicopter touched down, the back door was flung open and four big burly Federal agents exited. They all wore black suits, aviator sunglasses, and had the tell-tale ear-piece. *Fuckwits*, Christine thought. The agents formed a tight protective unit and one signaled.

The crowd gasped and the women oohed and aahed as President Aaron Sanderson stepped down. He was sporting a tan suit and looked immaculate. His suave jaw and cleft chin was almost cartoonish in the way it made him look and he used his smile to its full effect.

"Good morning!" he said cheerfully as he waved. The reporters rushed towards him, all holding out microphones or their cell phones.

"Thank you all for coming out on this wonderful day." His speech patterns sounded natural and yet also rehearsed. *Give him the Oscar*, Christine thought. "To be here, the first President of the United States to ever be invited to the prestigious Habanos Festival, is truly an honor. For this is a momentous occasion between two countries and there is much we can learn from both."

"Mr. President?" a British reporter started. "Is it true that the Russians are angered with the talks between Cuba and the USA?"

Another spoke up. "Some say that you are here to buy stock in Habanos S.A. Is that true?"

Sanderson smiled and held up his hands. Everyone hushed, except for the old crazy man Christine met on the bus. "Are you here to capture the War Profiteer Jeremiah Banks?"

The President ignored them as he flashed a million dollar smile. "Please. Please. Allow me to enjoy today and the fun activities ahead. Then, later tonight at the hotel, I will gladly answer any questions. Thank you."

He started to move and the agents followed. "You heard him. Back away now. After the tour, he will answer questions. Back away now!"

Christine watched as the small party of men made their way to an official-looking woman. She shook the president's hand then led them away. *Handles himself well*, she thought.

She quickly scanned the area and her eyes bulged.

"No fucking way!"

CHAPTER TEN

Since the arrival of President Sanderson, the area seemed to be swamped with tall, muscular gringos. Some were obviously agents while others had on the garb of turistas: ugly Hawaiian shirts, shorts and sneakers. To Christine, they were trying too hard to appear to be normal people.

What had made her exclaimed was the only man dressed for proper action. Military-grade cargo pants, boots, a light-weight short sleeve shirt and close-cut hair, Don stared at her, smiling brightly. He waved at her then blew a kiss.

Christine started to make her way through the crowd towards him, weaving and dodging the myriad of people, trying to get a glimpse of the president. Don kept moving too. They were playing Cat and Mouse. Unfortunately for him, Christine was not in the mood for a game.

Moving past a fat turista, she nimbly took his heavy SLR camera.

The nearer to Don Christine got, she started to wrap the heavy strap around her hand. The camera hung loosely, swaying gently from each step she took. Her hand tensed, followed by her arm. Eyes narrowing, Christine made sure there would be no one to get in the way. Her hand began to move in small circles, the strap twisting, camera spinning. The target? Back of the knees.

Don groaned loudly from the impact as his knees gave way. He dropped to the ground, landing on his palms then as he started to get to back up the fabric of the strap wrapped itself round his neck and he choked. The material cut into his skin as Christine kept pulling up.

"Up you get, darling," she whispered into his ear, yanking the man to his feet. His hands dove into his pockets, trying to find any weapon.

"Stop that, or you'll be dead."

He obeyed the command. Christine smiled, her eyes darting around, scanning to see if anyone had been witness to this brief scuffle. Satisfied, she tugged on the straps. "Right this way." Another sharp pull had Don being lead far from the crowd and into the stalks of tobacco.

Surrounded by the green, it reminded Christine of her training in Ireland. Wonderful times. The smell of the tobacco plants brought her back. Periodically, a veguero on a horse would gallop past them, on its way to another section of the plantation. Christine continued pulling the struggling man along the path between the plants. She was looking for a secluded patch of land.

Don tried to speak but all that came out was gurgles and splutters. Christine ignored him as she continued searching. Her eyes kept looking for signs of hats or voices. His hands started tapping her arms. Then they were hitting her.

She cried out from the stamp on her foot. The pain forced her to release her grip on the camera strap. Don elbowed her in the stomach and she dropped the camera. She kicked out at him and he dodged away.

They both stood there, panting and rubbing their sore parts. A breeze started the shoots swaying, causing the shadows to dance around them. The sun was almost at the noon point and the heat was sweltering. Christine was used to it.

"What the fuck are you doing here?" she asked between gulps for air.

"I could ask you the same," Don answered, eyes going to the camera that lay between them.

"Don't think about it," Christine warned, her own eyes at the camera.

"Too late."

They both dived at the same time, arms reaching out, fingers grasping. Don had the advantage. His arms were longer and the heavy slabs of meat he called hands wrapped around the strap.

Christine, on the other hand, had grabbed a clump of dirt. She threw it with all her might. Don screamed as a rock inside it split his nose, shattering the bone. His hands clamped to his face, trying to stop the blood flow. Christine was on her feet, the camera in her hand.

"Stupid, stupid monkey," she said as she wrenched one of his hands away from his face. She forced it behind Don's back and prised open the fingers. "We're going to have a little chat," she said casually.

"My nose! You broke my fucking nose!"

"Be quiet and speak when spoken to," Christine snapped as she slid the guillotine cutter down to the first knuckle of his ring finger. Gently, she closed the blades so that they were just touching his flesh. He stopped moving instantly.

"What's that?"

"This is what's going to happen," Christine said. "I'm going to ask questions. You will answer them. The moment you don't, well…" she closed the blades tighter. They started to cut the flesh.

"Okay! Okay! Okay!"

Christine chuckled. She was enjoying herself immensely. "First question. Where is Jeremiah Banks?"

"Who?"

It didn't take much pressure to slice the tip of the finger off. Don squealed like a stuck pig while he fought to get his hand back. Christine kneed him in the spine, causing him to double over. Quickly, the cutter went down to the next knuckle. "Once more. Where is Jeremiah Banks?"

"Fuck you! I don't know anything. I'm here on some point job. That's all!"

The blades once more started to close. The moment the metal touched his skin, "You crazy bitch! What do you want?"

"Just answer the question. Where is—?"

"—I don't know!" He begged. "You can't kill me!"

Christine laughed. "Why not?"

"Station Master would never back it."

"What?"

Don tried to turn his head so he could see her. He smiled. "You heard right."

"How do you know Station Master?"

"He brokered the deal for that drive and is bringing me into the Stat—"

A low moan escaped his lips as the next part of his finger was snipped away. Christine was careful to position the digit so that the blood would not hit her but just squirt onto the ground. "Why would Station Master bring you into the House?"

"I'm not going to say shit!" Don spat. "Take all my fingers." He laughed. "It doesn't matter. By the time this is all over, I'll be the new kid on the block and you… Why, you will be—"

Christine slammed the camera into the base of Don's skull. There was a sickening thud and the man fell forward. She then turned her head. The sounds of screaming and gunfire echoed across the plantation.

"It never ends," she muttered to herself, giving the unconscious Don a kick in the side.

#

Christine emerged from the stalks of tobacco to find herself surrounded by chaos. There were masked men all carrying AK-47s and spraying the area with bullets. This was an uncoordinated attack, her training said. The president and his team of agents were gone. Probably already made their escape. The helicopter was still on the ground, the pilot on his belly, blood oozing from a gash on the back of his head.

"Fucking great!" she muttered under her breath.

The closet thug heard her. Turning, he raised the weapon while shouting for her to get on the ground. Christine smiled. "Not a chance."

She ran full speed towards the man. He fumbled, startled that a woman would try to attack him. He raised the weapon then squeezed the trigger. An emotionless click. The AK had jammed. Christine dropped and slid across the earth, her hand flinging a handful of dust up at the man.

The thug dropped the weapon, clutching at his face. Christine scooped up the weapon by its barrel and with two swift smacks to the head, the man was down, unconscious.

Quickly, Christine slid the clip out, reloaded, pulled the stock back then took aim. Two short bursts and two other of the attackers laid dead. There were more out there. She could hear the shouts and clumsy firing. *Rank amateurs*, she thought.

As she moved forward, scanning the perimeter, Christine took up another two magazines. She kept one hugged against the clip in the AK, the other stuffed into her pants.

Christine moved with precision. Each time she got sight of another AK-45, her weapon sung. A short, sharp aria and they were dead. She was rusty, but not that rusty.

A hot searing pain ripped through her shoulder. Blood stained the earth and her hands. Whirling to her left, Christine emptied the clip into the assailant. He screamed as the bullets tore his lungs and heart to shreds. As the body collapsed, Christine had the second clip loaded and ready to go.

Christine followed the path of mewling turistas. All were on their stomachs in the dirt. It would've been funny, if not for the AK-47s ringing loud and clear. If only she knew how many were left. She could plan and do it right, not running in half-cocked guns all a-blazing.

Two of the masked thugs were dragging a veguero into the field of green. A quick scan and Christine was satisfied that these were the last ones, she hoped. Going into a dense vegetative growth with minimal field of view was definitely folly.

But she had to.

She slowed to a snail's pace. Each step had to be carefully chosen less she alerted them to her presence. She brushed against a stalk and as it swayed, the leaves brushed against another. And another. They moved one after another in a domino effect. She cursed herself.

"¿Qué fue eso?" she heard one say. They were to her right. Good. Now she had a general direction to go.

"¡Cállate!" the second said. It was followed by a smack and the veguero whimpered.

With as little noise as she could make, Christine raised the automatic rifle in her hands. She guessed where the thugs' heads were and then dropped the barrel two inches below that. *Better safe than sorry*, she thought.

Her finger twitched slightly on top of the trigger. She had to mentally focus her breathing. It was rapid and made the gun bounce ever-so-slightly. Christine closed her eyes and prayed that the veguero was short. Slowly, her trigger finger wrapped itself around the metal piece and then started to squeeze it.

There were screams of agony and pain as bullets rained from the sky. A helicopter was descending rapidly and from either side came the sounds of tracer rounds.

Christine ducked and covered her head. *It better not be the goddamn gringos*, she thought. If so, then the operation would be fucked. They would evacuate the president and Jeremiah Banks would be lost again, possibly forever. And she could not allow that.

It seemed an eternity for the rain of gunfire to cease. There would be a high chance that the tobacco in the area was lost, shredded and contaminated by the blood, flesh, muscle, sinew, and bone matter. Such a waste.

Slowly, Christine stood up.

The helicopter had landed, crushing stalks and bending others at ugly angles. There were men dressed in military garb and they all held small Uzis. Christine watched as some went over to the masked thugs and roughly checked the bullet-ridden bodies for any evidence. *Cuban paramilitary*, she thought, hoping for the best.

"Oye!" a familiar voice called to her from the helicopter. Juan de Dios waved at her. "Climb aboard, señora! I believe a lift is in order, eh?" He smiled and winked at her.

CHAPTER ELEVEN

"What the fuck was that?"

The helicopter had just taken off and Christine stared daggers at Juan. Far below them, more Cuban Intelligence agents had entered the area. They were taking care of the turistas and the reporters, making sure that no unwanted stories escaped into the Internet. That would be the last thing Cuba needed.

"Perdon?" Juan said distractedly. He was fiddling with the handle of his cane, twirling it this way then twisting it that. He seemed calm, completely at ease with the situation. It infuriated Christine more.

"You heard me, old man. That! Where was the team?"

"What team? I got no clearance to have any men there."

Christine's jaw dropped open. "No clearance? You're the fucking head of CI!"

"And?" he said matter of factly. "Just like you Christine, I too have a boss. It doesn't matter if I think a situation needs my attention. If our presidente says no, then no it will be. So it is written, so it shall be."

They both sat there in sullen silence. Christine looked out at the vast field of tobacco. It was beautiful and made her feel slightly better. Then her eyes spotted something and she squinted.

It was the army. They had cleared a circle in the middle of the tobacco, dug a mass grave, and then she watched as they started to dump the bodies into it. "Juan, what are they doing?"

The old man shrugged nonchalantly. "What the army does best. Clean up messes."

Christine sighed in frustration. The old man's attitude was beginning to annoy her more and more. Her eyes went back to the disappearing fields and she gasped. Large plumes of black smoke were billowing up from the hole. The army had obviously used flamethrowers to burn the dead.

"Why…?"

Juan sighed. "To stop the spread of the disease. That is the only way to make sure the entire island is safe."

Christine's mind raced. *The disease? Is it linked to what I saw earlier?* "What disease? Should I be worried?"

Juan de Dios shook his head. "That's classified."

That was it. Christine had had enough. "Classified my ass, Juan! You are the head of CI. You decide what is and is not classified."

"Used to," he said with an air of defeat.

The situation in Cuba had changed more than Christine knew. "What happened?" she asked. "You were completely separate. Now you need permission to have surveillance? Por favor!"

The old spy master laughed dryly. "Since President Sanderson, the government has wanted to show the gringos that they can play by their rules. So everything has slowly become like them. Government bodies were the first."

"I thought CI was outside the government," she said.

Another laugh from the Cuban. "Was. Shortly after Sanderson started talking to Esposito, the mandate came down that our budget would be slashed if we didn't agree to certain new…ways of doing things."

"Like what?"

"Answering to a government liaison. That's just one of the problems we face now."

"Puta madre," she exclaimed.

Juan nodded as the helicopter continued its flight. "It doesn't help that the liaison is a real marica." He held a cigar in his hand, pondering if it was worth lighting. It wasn't. "She came recommended by the gringo ambassador, which I thought was funny. But, she seems to be working out okay."

"You've lost your huevos!" Christine said. "Back in the old days—"

"The old days are dead and gone," he retorted, "and if you're not careful, you will be too."

The helicopter bounced up and down from turbulence. Christine held tightly to the seat. "What does that mean?"

"¿En serio? Come on, Christine! There's only one reason Station Master would send someone like you here and it's not to complete a mission."

"Fuck you, Juan."

Juan de Dios shook his head sadly. "Always blinded by duty, my dear. One day, it will get you killed."

"Maybe," she said. "Maybe not. Maybe fuck you and anyone dumb enough to try."

She looked out at the countryside. It was beautiful and always had been. "At least tell me something, Juan."

"Anything."

"Why didn't you have any people at Pinar del Rio today? You knew that Sanderson would be there. If it had been me, that's where I would have done the deed."

"The liaison said it would have too many witnesses and that there are more likely targets that we should check out," Juan said after a moment. "Plus, there was a big agent. Called himself Don, I think. He said he would have the president covered... I didn't see him."

Christine tried to look innocent, but came off looking smug. "We had some unfinished business. I needed to balance the books."

"Hijo de puta!" Juan spat. "He was the go-to agent for us! What have you done?"

Temper rising, Christine had to bite her tongue. "My job is to protect the president of the United States from any threat. That man was a threat when I first met him. He will always be a threat to me. If you have a problem with that, then you can go to hell!"

"You are a silly girl. That's why you got your agents killed," Juan said calmly. "You let your emotions lead you, not your mind. Think, Christine! Be rational. That is the skill we have. Our minds are our greatest weapon. That is why you will never be like Station Master or myself."

They sat in silence. All that could be heard was the rotor

blades cutting through the air. Juan looked as if he had given a sermon upon the mount while Christine had the expression of a child. Havana was fast approaching them.

"Maybe," she said as the helicopter started to descend, "I don't want to be anything like you. Maybe, I want my own life at some point."

"Then you shouldn't have gotten involved in this life."

"Maybe you should..." she stopped herself. "What can you tell me about the attackers?"

Juan sighed. "Finally," he said. "Dominicans and Haitians most likely. They pop up here periodically when dirty deeds need to be done, though it's odd that they would be working together."

"But why? It was so slap-shot and uncoordinated."

He nodded his head. "Indeed. Not credible at all. But, what's interesting are the weapons."

"Goat horns, I know," she said, using the old nickname for AK-47s. "Where would they have gotten them?"

Juan shrugged. "Plenty of the old guard would have some stashed away. Why, my mother has four under her mattress. I keep saying to her, 'Mama they are why your back is crooked.' And she says 'Si, niño, but at least I sleep well.'" He laughed. "My mother is a wise lady."

"Aren't all mothers," Christine asked.

"Indeed. But, they had been serviced recently, which leads this old man to believe that there is someone in Havana that wants to cause problems."

Christine stared at the man; her expression said it all: No shit.

"I know, my dear, but, we must be thorough. I've already started a list of the usual suspects."

"Is Jeremiah Banks on that list?"

Juan coughed as the helicopter landed.

"I thought so. Why isn't anyone taking him seriously?"

"We are and have. But he is a—"

"Ghost now. Si, everyone's been saying that."

They clambered out of the vehicle. Christine had to help Juan down. "How am I supposed to get back to the Nacional?"

#

The Cadillac Coup Deville raced along the dirt roads. Juan

looked younger driving it while Christine had to hold on for dear life. They had landed somewhere outside of Havana. For security, she had been told, and now they were in Juan's pride and joy. He had said that he would be more than glad to give her a lift.

"I do love driving. The fresh air. The scenery. It makes me feel alive," Juan was saying with glee. "At my age, there isn't much that can do that."

Christine chuckled, more to make him feel better than because he was being witty. "Can you get Jeremiah Banks? Arrest him or detain him."

The car swerved to miss an old man and his son walking along the road. "Why do you keep bringing him up? Leave the past in the past."

"This isn't about then. Station Master's intel said that Banks was behind this."

They entered the city, driving through New New Havana, where some gringo money had already started to build modern monstrosities. "Pinche gringos," Juan said. "They come here with their money claiming to want to keep Havana pure and look at these!"

"Don't change the subject," Christine said as the car sped up. They passed through New New Havana quickly then into New Havana. The moment they had crossed the imaginary border, Juan breathed again.

"Perdóname," he said, "what were you saying?"

"Intel. The Station's intel said that Jeremiah Banks is the one behind this. Can you get him for me?"

Juan chuckled. "The Station's intel? Show me this intel, Christine. Here in Cuba, we have heard no word of Señor Banks in a very long time. You'll have a better chance of finding WMDs at the Bay than him."

Christine sunk into her chair slightly at that. This was the second time that someone had mentioned WMDs at Guantanamo. *Adriana had better come back with news or heaven help her*, she thought. This better not be some wild goose chase Station Master was sending her on. So far, there had be no concrete evidence that Jeremiah Banks was involved. If that was the case, then this was a suicide mission.

"...who can say what intel is legitimate and what isn't, eh?" Juan was saying. "With the Internet and modern technology, everyone can have a say. Now, I'm not saying that Station Master is wrong. But the Station's reputation has been sullied. What? You thought we didn't know. First Havana. Then there was that episode in Australia. Serbia. Egypt. What next?"

"We all make mistakes, Juan."

"But that many in such a short time? No, my dear. After a while, the mind goes. Station Master is old. It was bound to happen. This is most likely a last-ditch attempt at saving face. I wouldn't be surprised if the only people trying to kill Sanderson are the Muslims again."

He hummed happily as they sped along the Malecón. Christine was furious. Damn both old men for their cocky ways. She'd show them. Christine Moore was not a mere child. She knew things and didn't have to just rely on her gut.

As the Nacional's cupolas came into view, Christine had an idea, "Do you know where Sanderson is going to be tonight?"

"The Saratoga. The pendejo thought the Nacional was too old fashioned," he spat out the window.

"Thanks, Juan. One more question."

The car had stopped in front of the Nacional. Christine felt more calm being back at the hotel. "Tomorrow, what's his agenda?"

"A tour of the old Partagas factory... Christine, tell me you are not planning to do anything stupid?"

Christine got out of the car and smiled at the old Cuban. "Ask your contact."

She went up and entered the hotel, ignoring Juan's calls.

CHAPTER TWELVE

Back in her hotel room, Christine is furious, even though she has an idea. How Adriana and Juan have been treating her, acting as if they have nothing to do with each other; talking to Christine as if she was nothing more than a new agent fresh from training. *Fuck them in the ass*, she thought. *And damn Don too! No way Station Master would recruit him, right?*

No, it didn't matter. She had a job to do. Stop a presidential assassination and capture Jeremiah Banks. One was easy. The other so far was proving nigh on impossible.

"Remember what Station Master said," she talked to herself as she went through her small collection of clothes, "break everything down into steps. Easy to do steps." She nodded as she picked out an elegant night dress with red and blue colors. "Step one, stop the assassination. Easy."

Christine laid out the dress on the bed then caught a look at herself in the mirror. She was sweaty, dirty, and in need of a shower.

"Rafael? It's Christine. Please tell me there is hot water available" she asked into the phone.

"Si, Christine. Planning a night out, eh?"

She giggled slightly. "Just a visit to the Saratoga."

"Oh," the voice was sullen, "not betraying our lady, I trust?"

"Good lord no! Just working."

"Ah, well then. Enjoy yourself and happy hunting!"

She hung up then went to the shower. She stared at herself in the mirror as the water ran, waiting for it to heat up sufficiently.

She admired her muscles and skin tones. She had always liked her boobs and the curves and naturalness of them. The scars on the other hand, they reminded her of all the mistakes of the past. The small scar just above her hip, the Istanbul job. The screen door on her thigh, Mombasa. The scar that caused the most pain was the one that ran down between her breasts. That was the reminder of Cuba. What happens when you let your heart lead. It was long and ugly looking, like a snake had been carved into her and it was a darker shade.

Whenever she had to be intimate during a job, this was always something she had been worried about. The rest of the scars were fine. But this? *Granted*, she thought, *there hadn't been many assignments where she had to get naked*. But the worry was still there. A great ass, pretty eyes, and acrobatic skills in the bedroom would only get her so far.

She tried putting the thoughts out of her mind as she slipped into the shower, letting the warm water wash over her, cleansing her of the day's sins. God, she needed this. It didn't take long for her to clean up. Her hair took the longest. She had to look perfect after all, if she wanted a meeting with President Sanderson.

After the shower, a quick dry and she had slipped into the dress, Christine took a moment to admire herself. It was form fitting and hugged her in all the right places. Her hair she did in a lovely ponytail. A silver hair band placed in it was the finishing touch. "That'll do, pig," she said to herself.

\#

The Hotel Saratoga sits across the Capitol Building and is one of those classic hotels one must see at some point. It has been there since 1933 when it moved from Monte Street. Sporting a classic art deco exterior, this is one of the key hotels for local bands to play and for dignitaries to visit, if they are after a slightly more modern feel. There is some debate as to whether the Nacional is better. For some it is. Traditionalists always say so.

Christine paid the driver as she got out of the taxi. It sped away quickly, looking for the next fare. She wiped her dress, trying to smooth out the wrinkles. The men in the immediate area tried to be subtle while checking her out. They failed. The women on the other hand were more successful, but Christine knew this was going to happen. She pulled her dress up so the tail wouldn't be dragged through the dirt, and she started walking up the steps to the entrance.

As she got nearer, Christine slowed her pace and cursed herself for being stupid. There were security checkpoints at all the entrances. Metal detectors, body scanners, and armed Federal agents were checking everyone who entered. *Of course they would have these*, she scolded herself. *There wouldn't be any chance of getting into the hotel, let alone the penthouse suite.* She watched as a fat Brazilian with a hooker on his arm try to talk his way into the foyer and then was promptly thrown out.

Christine scanned the area, looking for any way to get in. If not, then she would have to contact Juan and hope he still had enough clout to get herself in. But after their fight earlier, it didn't seem likely. It reminded her of Mombasa; the head of the local agency did everything he could to hinder her actions. *No fucking way*, she thought. Then her eyes caught a glimpse of something and she smiled.

A small bus, actually a van, had pulled up on the corner and exiting it were a gaggle of Cuban floozies, most likely prostitutes. All were dressed scantily with heavy makeup on and pointing at the roof of the hotel. The pimp started hustling them towards the first checkpoint and Christine knew how she could get in.

#

The elevator dinged open and the floozies rushed for the first available wealthy man they could find. This is standard operating procedure for escorts as it means they can latch on to a gentleman and siphon their funds all night long. Only one took her time.

Her dress looked slightly torn like the owner had taken a pair of scissors to it. To the fashionably inclined, it was the latest style. Grunge they called it. Her eyes were smoky and her lips were red. Deep red. Almost to a heightened style. Christine admired the view. The Capitol building was lit up and seemed like the perfect beacon of hope for Cuba. She knew better.

Around her was a hedonist's paradise. Three small open bars with the finest selections of rum, tequila, and some whisky. There was a small dance floor that was packed to the brim with girls dancing, laughing, and having a drunken fun time. Christine shook her head. The elevator dinged again and the doors started to slide shut. She gracefully glided out and into the unwashed throng.

The music was Cuban but with a hint of the most vilest of music genres known to Latin America. Reggaeton. *Whoever had decided on this music should be drawn and quartered*, she chuckled to herself. A slightly drunk frat boy type came up to her with a big glass of a vile-looking concoction. "Hey beaut'ful, how about a drinshk?" he slurred, holding out the beverage.

Christine shook her head. "Not right now, baby, I'm looking for my papi."

She moved away from the guy who within seconds was hooking up with a barely dressed woman.

As Christine moved along the rooftop, her eyes kept scanning for the president. Where the hell could he be? She didn't have time for a wild goose chase.

"And then! Then! I slapped her ass and sent her back to the secretary pool!" She heard the boisterous laugh which was followed by uncomfortable chuckles. "Now, who wants a presidential inspection?"

There he was. President Aaron Sanderson in the pool, surrounded by naked women. All were drinking and trying to get his attention. The man himself was smoking a large Cohiba with one arm around the closest body and the other holding a large beer. He was laughing, smoking, and trying to nuzzle her bosom at the same time. It was going to end in tears.

Which it did.

The cigar touched the breast, and the woman cried out, quickly moving away, ducking under the water to soothe the slight burn. When she came up, she was swearing in rapid Español. "English! Say it in fucking goddamn proper English!" the President snapped. His smoke was ruined and he tossed it away disgusted.

So this was the leader of the supposed free world, Christine mused. Definitely living up to all the stories. She watched as the President snapped his fingers, getting the attention of the nearest agent who rushed over then bent down and listened. Seconds later, three agents had grabbed the woman and escorted her to the elevator, sans clothes.

Sanderson roared with laughter at the sight but was quickly distracted by a fresh cigar and fresh body. "Fuck me I love this country! Everything is ripe for the taking," he exclaimed, "and I do mean ripe." He growled as his free hand fondled the young lady who was faking her pleasure sounds. These pros must have been getting paid a pretty sum of money.

"Yes, that's the leader of the free world," a gruff voice said next to Christine. She turned slightly and smiled. Next to her stood a squat agent. His bearing was that of a man who knows his position and how to defend it. "Don't worry," he said, "I'm not going to try anything. You just seem like a normal woman." He shrugged as he said this, uncomfortable with small talk.

"I thought he would be more…refined," Christine said, trying to sound dumb and failing.

"In public yeah. But…you know the saying, absolute power corrupts."

They stood there watching the debacle before them. It was obvious that at any moment the President would either drown or get a knee to the crotch, in which case the party would be over.

"Are you head of security?"

The agent nodded. "You have something to report?"

Christine swallowed. This would be her only chance. "I have information about a possible attempt on the President's life."

"We get those three times a day."

"Maybe but," Christine said as she moved in front of the agent so she could see his face properly. It was craggy and had seen much violence. "This comes from the most dangerous man in Cuba. I can tell you everything. Just let me speak to the President."

The agent glared at her; that seemed to be his only emotion. His mind was ticking over and each second more made Christine nervous. She didn't want to be kicked out before she could warn the President.

Then, "Okay, you'll have five minutes with him. Any funny business and I'll put a bullet through that pretty face."

#

The penthouse suite had been refurnished, probably for the President. It reeked of new money and the shininess of capitalism. *Fidel would be rolling in his grave*, Christine thought as she tried to make herself comfortable. The agent had led her in, told her the rules then left promptly saying that he'd be back with the president.

That was five minutes ago as far as she could tell. She would wait another ten and then leave, making sure there would be a note for him to find. It would be a futile effort on her part, but at least she would have warned him, in a fashion.

The small alarm clock also had a radio in it, as most do nowadays. *Even in Havana*, she thought, *they need to keep up certain appearances*. The radio was on and the gentle song had just ended leading into a news report. She listened intently.

"...in the south. I repeat there are reports of strange and horrific incidents happening in the south and eastern parts of our beloved Cuba. In Trinidad, there have been at least fifty cases of family members attacking others and... I'm sorry listeners, but I can't believe what I'm reading. Cannibals. Cuba has cannibals! Also, it appears that in the mountains of the Sierra Maestra the... Is this a joke? En serio?!... Okay... There are reports of the dead... I'm sorry! But zombies are not real!"

Christine shook her head and tried to be logical about what she had seen and now heard. It was hard; her training and rationality screamed at her not to believe that there was a zombie plague hitting Cuba. *No*, she told herself, *get the proof first*. She turned her attention back to the radio.

"...I apologize for my earlier outburst. But, this is the most unbelievable news I have had to report to you in my thirty years of being on air. If these reports are an elaborate hoax, then the person or persons responsible will be caught and prosecuted. Until then, our illustrious Presidente has declared that our beloved Cuba is in a State of Emergency. It pains me to say this but... There is a plague in Cuba."

The door swung open and as Christine spun to face it, President Sanderson walked in. He was wearing a bathrobe and seemed pissed. "What the fuck do you mean, Harris?" he was saying to the agent. "I had my pick of the tits and ass up there. Why would you pull me away from that...hello beautiful!" He smiled creepily the moment he saw her. "What can I do for you? An autograph perhaps? A picture?"

He moved towards her, arms reaching out, trying to grasp her. Christine moved away quickly and made the decision to keep a chair between herself and the horny President.

"Mister President," she began "I have information about your safety in Cuba."

"Harris!" the President barked. "How did you get this beauty? She reminds me of my daughter," and he growled lustily.

"President Sanderson! Your life is at risk here," Christine continued. "A man called Jeremiah Banks is planning to kill you, before the end of the festival."

Sanderson wasn't paying attention though. His eyes were on Christine's body. "Come here, sweetheart. Tell the President all about it." He licked his lips as he circled towards her. "And who knows, maybe we could discuss another important matter of state," as he said this, he untied the robe and let it slip off.

Christine tried to avoid looking at the naked man. The agent had disappeared; apparently, this was a standard technique for them. "Mister President, this is serious!"

The man nodded. "I believe you. This is very serious." He wiggled his erect member at her. "Come here and make me understand." He grinned at her lecherously.

Another idea came to Christine. She smiled sweetly at him. "Sure thing, Papi," she said, "but first, what will you do about the killer? Cancel all public appearances?"

The President laughed as she started walking towards him. "How about you convince me, my dear. I'm used to getting death threats."

Christine nodded and reached out a hand towards the President. She would have to act quickly and make him understand, the drunk misogynist.

"If you were to cancel all public engagements while here, I would be yours until you leave, and I can make you feel pleasure like you have never felt before."

The President shuddered as she gently wrapped her fingers around him. "Go on," he breathed.

"Promise you'll stay indoors. Or at least use a double," she whispered into his ear.

"What about my popularity?"

"I'm your popularity."

A scream escaped from the President as Christine wrenched the member. She twisted it and pulled it in directions it was not meant to go. "You listen to me," she said, all business. "If you don't stop this and take my advice, then you'll be dead. The USA will go to war with Cuba which will bring Russia into it and World War Three will start."

The President of the United States screamed again as Christine wrenched once more. Christine could hear banging on the door and muted voices calling for the President. *Time to go*, she thought.

"Think about it, Papi," she said with disdain and gave one final hard pull. She let go, kicked the President in the crotch, and made her way to the door as he collapsed, unconscious.

She opened the door and left with a smile.

#

Outside, she shivered. The night had been a waste of time and Christine felt the urge to beat someone. Anyone. The first person to cross her. She hoped it would be a man. At that moment, she felt a burning hatred towards all men.

"Disculpe, señora," a small voice said to her.

Looking down, Christine saw a little girl. She held a folded piece of paper. The girl looked at her and held the paper up. "I was told to give this to you."

"Gracias, niña," Christine said and as she took the paper, she gave the girl a small handful of pesos. The girl smiled then ran away into the night.

Christine looked around trying to see who would have sent the note. There was nobody suspicious looking. Slowly, she unfolded the note:

GO TO PAPA'S. THERE YOU WILL FIND WHAT YOU SEEK.

Right, Christine thought as she used her lighter to burn the piece of paper.

CHAPTER THIRTEEN

Ernest Hemingway loved Cuba. He lived, wrote, drank, fought, smoked, and fished there. His most famous piece of work, The Old Man and The Sea, was written there.

There are many places that purportedly say that Hemingway visited drank or was there for an extended period of time. It is hard to distinguish the man from the myth. But for Cuba, it is one hell of a business.

Papa's was created to capitalize on the famed author's reputation. The menu and drink list are all supposedly the food and beverages that Hemingway loved while living in Havana. The decor is inspired by Hemingway House and the artifacts are either replicas or fakes. Nobody cares though; it is the spot for Hemingway enthusiasts.

Why on earth would a small restaurant have any answers for Christine though? She had to find out. It was late and she was getting tired of all the dead ends. Eventually, something would have to break in the case or she would have to call Station Master and then there would be hell to pay.

Any lead was worth following up on, she told herself as she stood in front of the small house that had been converted into the restaurant. The sign was a replica of Hemingway's signature that had written his nickname, Papa's. There were no people waiting to get in which was odd. At this time of night during the Habanos Festival, every restaurant and bar was packed. This was suspicious.

Christine slowly went up the small stairs then ducked to the right, using the door jam for cover, just in case. She tried to peer in through the windows, but the curtains were drawn. The lights were on, that she was sure about. Damn, if only she had a gun or knife. Without them, going into an unknown location and situation was idiotic, but she had to risk it. Adriana and Juan were being useless.

Slowly, she reached out and touched the doorknob. It wasn't hot and didn't feel funny. Gently, she turned it. The door swung open silently. Christine felt uneasy. This was too simple.

Bending down, she checked to see if there was a trip wire. Nothing. Instead, she found a footprint that was the color of blood. The sense of unease started to change becoming dread. Standing, Christine gently stepped over the bloody imprints of boots. There were multiple tracks. At least three that she could count.

Inside the main area, a living room and dining room that had been joined and then converted into the restaurant proper, there were bullet holes pockmarking the walls, ceiling and floor. Around some tables were pools of blood. No bodies though. Christine grabbed a large steak knife and held it at the ready. It would do nada against a trained opponent, but it was the best she could do.

She continued walking through the restaurant, stepping on any part of the floor that was not covered in pools of blood. She noticed that the puddles of blood had streaks, as if the body or bodies of the dead had been dragged. Christine sniffed the air; burning food. She quickened her steps.

The streaks of blood parted into two paths, one heading to the back of the building, the other went towards the smell. It was the kitchen.

Treading carefully, Christine used the point of the blade to push open the swing door that led into the kitchen.

"Jesus!" she exclaimed.

The burning smell came from the grill where the two cooks had their heads sizzling nicely. They were burnt and some would say overdone. The hands had been tied to each other and to either side of the metal cooker. Christine's first instinct was to turn off the grill, but her training kicked in; better to be observant than cause problems. The rest of the kitchen staff had been lined up against a wall then executed. The large butcher knives and chef knives were buried deep into the bodies.

Quickly, Christine exited the kitchen then made her way to the back, keeping to the side of the hallway, knife still at the ready. Her heart was beating faster and faster at each step. She had a rough idea of what was behind the door and a part of her screamed not to open it. But she had to. There were answers here.

A swift kick and the door slammed open. Christine stared at the mass of bodies heaped before her. Men, women, and children. Their faces forever locked in expressions of screams, disbelief, and anguish. Knives impaled into faces, skin burnt off, bullet-ridden bodies.

"Dios mio," Adriana said softly.

Christine whirled around, her blade flashing brightly as she brought it up. The slice was quick and Adriana had to be quicker. She dodged it then caught the next attack. "Chris! It's me!"

Adriana disarmed the other woman then gently sat the knife on a table. She took Christine's hand and led her back to the main room.

"What happened here?" she asked.

Christine shook her head. "I got a note saying that I would find answers here. All I found was this."

"Do you know who sent you the note?"

Adriana watched as Christine shook her head. "A girl gave it to me… What are you doing here?"

"My section got an anonymous tip about yelling and screaming. I got over here as soon as I could. You were not what I was expecting." She stood and started looking around. Christine sat, staring at her hands.

"Chris, you better see this." The call brought Christine back to the present.

Slowly, she got to her feet then made her way back to the mass of bodies in the back.

Adriana had started to shift the bodies but had stopped. She was a couple of steps away and pointing. Christine stood at the door. Her eyes followed the finger to the pile of bodies. There were new faces and one in particular made Christine's heart sink.

In life, he had been fun and loyal and always pleasant. But now, Rafael Cienfuentes was nothing more than a body, a lifeless vessel. There were four bullet holes in his chest and his face had been beaten. Where once was a nose, now there was a pulpy mess.

"They really went to town on him, eh?"

"What the hell was he doing here?" Christine asked.

"You know him?" Adriana was surprised. "I just wanted to show you, this was the guy they were after. I mean, look at how they treated him compared to the rest."

Christine wasn't listening. She had leaned down and was staring at the bloody mess. "He was the manager at the Nacional."

"Why would he be here then?" Adriana asked. "What could he know that would get him killed?"

Christine stood then looked at the other woman. "You tell me," she said quietly.

Before Adriana could reply, she had been grabbed by the hair and forcefully dragged back into the main room. Christine flung her into a chair.

Adriana was back on her feet with her fists up.

"What the fuck was that, you stupid cunt?"

Christine took a moment and breathed in. Slowly, she turned to face Adriana. "That body in there was CI. You should know that."

"You attack me because I don't know some low-level lackey? Grow the fuck up, Chris." Adriana laughed. "You should know by now that not everyone in an agency knows someone else. It's the way of the fucking world."

"Then tell me something," Christine said as she started to look around the restaurant.

"Hang on," Adriana said, cutting her off. "What are you doing?"

Christine stopped turned and stared daggers at the Cuban. "Looking for clues. Now, you want to help?"

Adriana nodded and the two of them started to rummage through the wreckage. "Why would a concierge be murdered?" Adriana asked herself.

"Probably knew something he wasn't supposed to."

"But what?" Adriana's tone wasn't that of someone needing to know a secret; more of someone hoping to stop a secret from getting out.

"If I knew," Christine replied, "then I wouldn't be looking through a trash bin."

They continued searching in the kitchen. "Let's look at this logically," began Adriana. "He was CI, right? He worked at the Nacional where a lot of important people stayed. He'd have access to lots of dirty secrets. Maybe he saw or heard something he shouldn't have."

"Doubt it," Christine replied as she started to make her way to the back room.

"Where you going?"

Christine didn't turn her head as she said, "Checking the body. Might be something there."

Adriana rushed to follow the woman.

When she got there, she saw Christine, all business, pulling the body away from the pile. It was hard work and by the end of it Christine was sweating. "Why don't you check the other bodies?" she said as she started to check Rafael's pockets.

With deliberate slowness, Adriana went to the first body she could find and made a show of checking it. Her eyes never left Christine's hands. "What if we don't find anything? I should call this in and get the policia involved. You're leaving clues everywhere and if they suspect you—"

"What do we have here?" Christine asked as she held up a small notebook. Adriana watched as Christine flipped the book open to the felt marker. Christine read the page, blinked, reread it, and blinked once more then turned to Adriana.

"Spill it. Now," she said as she held up the book for Adriana to see.

It read:

Guantánamo es un callejón sin salida.

CHAPTER FOURTEEN

"So while you were having fun gallivanting around Pinar del Rio," Adriana started as they sat on the front step, both puffing away on cigars, "I made the long, long trip to the Bay. Have you been? It's really quite lovely. If you ignore the military compound that is," she giggled, trying to lighten the mood. Christine stared out into the inky darkness.

Adriana cleared her throat and took another draw on the stogie then continued. "So, I get there, and there are military police everywhere. I've never seen so many big men with weapons in my life." An evil grin spread across her face.

"Focus, Adriana."

"Oh, si. Naturalmente… As I was saying. Military police all over, so I need to figure out how to get in."

"What about your contact?"

Adriana blinked. "Well, I had no idea if he was there. Either way, I would have to improvise and you know how much I love to do that," she chuckled as Christine rolled her eyes. "There aren't many ways to get in without an official ID and since CI is a clandestine agency, I couldn't very well just tell them who I am. Also doesn't help what with the Bay technically being US land. It certainly wasn't going to be easy, believe you me."

"Get on with it," Christine snapped.

"Testy today, aren't we?" Adriana replied. "Are we sure it isn't that special time?"

"You know what," Christine asked as she stood. "I don't need your shit. Now or ever. If you are not going to get to the point and tell me…fine! I'll go myself." She stood before the Cuban spy, nostrils flaring, barely controlling her frustrations. Adriana giggled, then laughed. Christine could not believe it.

"Bravo!" Adriana clapped loudly. "An amazing performance. No really. Better than Gabo. Take a bow." She shook her head. "Jesus, Christine. You really have forgotten how things are done Cuba."

"You fuck me and then fuck me over. I remember clearly." Christine's tone was flat.

Adriana flinched. "Not that…sorry…maldita sea…you know…" She stopped talking, closed her eyes then took a deep breath. "What I meant was that us Cubans love telling a good story."

"I don't have time for a story. I need the facts."

"Can we get out of here," Adriana said, deflecting Christine's statement. "The policia should really take care of this… How about the Nacional?"

Christine shook her head. "The facts. Now."

Adriana sighed then stared at her cigar. "Fine. But first, I never fucked you over."

Christine scoffed. "Really?"

"We all have to do shitty things for the job. You too. Don't pretend that you are the innocent in all this. I did what I had to do for my country."

"Bullshit," Christine cut in. "You did what you had to do for money. Cold hard cash. Provided by Jeremiah Banks. Why? Tell me that!"

Adriana sat there, her eyes big and watery. Christine paced up and down the small garden. The cigar acting like a chimney for her. "Why else? To get ahead in life."

"But my men! My reputation!" Christine tried to sound indignant but deep down she knew that Adriana was right. She would have done the exact same thing, on orders or on her own. This was a nasty business to be involved in and each year it seemed to be getting worse for Christine.

Adriana looked as if she could read Christine's thoughts. "You would have done the same."

Christine took what could be counted as an eternity before she slowly nodded her head. The other woman smiled slightly. A minor victory is still a victory.

"Sit, Chris," Adriana said, patting the spot next to her. "You're going to like this. Or hate it." She smiled properly as Christine almost collapsed next to her.

"I won't bore you with how I got in…unless you want to know? Well, to sum it up, I told them I worked for the Cuban Government as their liaison between the FBI and CI. They didn't believe me at first. The guards looked as if they were going to throw me into one of those cells they use for rendition." She shuddered slightly. "I put on my best smile, you know the one. Big moist, ruby red lips. Completely inviting. I told them to call the Cuban Minister of Defense and ask him if a Teresa Guadalupe Luna was conducting inspections during the President's visit. They did." She held up the cigar and stared at the ash. Gently, she tapped the wrapper, and the ash floated to the ground where it disappeared.

"That is the stupidest name I have ever heard!" Christine finally laughed. "Like something out of James Bond."

"Well, it worked. They called the Minister who was having lunch with Juan at the time so everything went like clockwork. They let me in and had some young administration officer play tour guide. This poor man didn't know anything about the facility, just all the usual PR lies. So, I had to ditch him."

"Naturally."

Adriana nodded. "I fed him some bull about women problems and he led me to the toilet. I went in, waited the appropriate amount of time, and then asked him for assistance. The dummy actually came in. Then I used my feminine wiles to distract him, stole his security card, and sent him back to the office with a smile and a kiss. Brilliant tactic, wouldn't you say?"

Christine shook her head. "I wouldn't. This sounds too easy. Even by gringo standards."

"Yeah, I thought so too, but then my Abuelo's saying came to mind. 'Suspicion leads to loneliness and a dead dog.' He was an odd man. But anyway… Where was I? Oh, si! After ditching the boy, I had to get to the lower levels. They aren't on any maps, but

CI has the original blueprints. Did you know Cuba used to get paid by the US for the land Guantanamo is on? Like renting. Fidel told them to go fuck themselves."

"Adriana," Christine said, "stay on target."

"Si si si si si. The lower levels. I was able to get past the security cameras and most of them, but there were two of the biggest baddest Danny Trejoest guards you have ever seen and they were always behind me. It got really annoying after a while. Once I got to an elevator, it was fine. Used the card and went straight to the sub-basement. According to the blueprints in the late 70s, the gringos built another base on top of the old bunker embedded in the ground. I know! It's all so fascinating. So, they built this base on top of where the nukes were supposed to be."

"What do you mean 'supposed to be,'" Christine asked. Her eyes narrowed as she jumped ahead, figuring out the ending before the final reel.

"Well, the rumors of WMDs at the Bay is laughable to begin with. Who would plant bombs here? The Russians? Well maybe." She pulled a face. "The gringos? I doubt it. See, CI has never put much stock in the tales of WMDs but, because of our relationship with The Station, we had to go and check it out. Just for you, really."

"I'm honored."

Adriana chuckled and stood. "You hungry? How about we get some food?"

"After you finish your report."

"So serious. Well, I got to the sub-basement and spent the longest time tapping on the walls, looking for any cracks with hints of air flow. I was getting bored, Chris. I couldn't find any traces of secret rooms, launch areas, nukes, or biological weapons." Adriana shook her head. "I'm sorry but there are no WMDs on Cuba."

Christine stood up. "Bullshit! Really?"

"En serio. I even spoke to my contact who sent me every old document to go through. That's what I was doing before I got the call to come here. Never in the history…well, except the Missile Crisis, has there been any nuclear devices on the island. The old bunker at Guantanamo was a granary. Then when the US moved in, they realized what they had on their hands and..." She held her hands up; the story was over.

"Damnit!" Christine said. "What's his game?"

"Whose?"

"Jeremiah Banks! If it isn't nukes, then why would he want to assassinate the President... is there even a plot?"

Adriana stood up then took the other woman's hands. "You need to take a moment, Chris. When was the last time you ate?"

#

"Eaten," Christine repeated, surprised at the audacity of the question. "We are standing in front of a massacre and you want me to eat?"

"Tranquilo," Adriana started to say but a moan from inside Papa's stopped her. "What was that?"

Again, the moan sounded, but this time they could tell where it came from. Christine and Adriana exchanged startled looks. "Kitchen," Adriana whispered.

Christine's eyes grew wide. "Rafael?"

They both trampled into the building, their cigars dropping on to the ground, forgotten. As they passed the main dining room, Christine saw, from her peripheral, that some of the bodies were twitching slightly. *No time for that*, she told herself. Her primary target was checking on her friend.

In the kitchen, Christine nearly knocked over Adriana. "What the fuck, Adri—?" she stopped mid-sentence when she saw the look of absolute horror on the Cuban woman's face. She was pointing at something and when Christine's gaze followed it, she too almost screamed.

For trying to free itself from the pile of now writhing and moaning bodies was Rafael. At least, it looked like him. The structure of the face, apart for the pulpy nose, was his, as were the clothes. But the eyes, they were definitely not his. Where once there was life and joy now only blank nothingness and hunger showed.

"What the fuck?" Christine whispered as the creature continued to crawl towards the two ladies. The fingernails were cracked and each time it dragged itself, the nails became more and more cracked and ruined until one by one they were torn off.

"You don't see that every day," Adriana commented as she studied the crawling corpse.

"So far I have. Twice."

The Cuban chuckled as she bent down. She tilted her head and looked into the face of the undead manager of the Hotel Nacional. "Anyone in there?"

A snarl escaped from the mouth and then with flapping of arms, it popped free of the pile, which caused the rest of the bodies to shudder and collapse, spreading across the floor. Instinctively, Christine stepped backwards as Adriana stayed exactly where she was. Slowly, Rafael's corpse shambled to its feet and stood unsteadily, swaying slightly. The head tilted to the side as if it was questioning everything it was seeing. The pale skin was almost translucent and the veins were visible. The eyes were nothing more now than orbs of pale gray.

"Rafael," Christine whispered softly in despair. At the sound of his name, the undead man turned his head towards her. Something must've clicked in the remains of the brain and step by shaky step, the creature went for Christine.

Adriana stood up and moved in front of the disgusting creature. The walking corpse's hair was matted down and the skin seemed to ooze liquid. "¿Dónde crees que vas, señor," she asked, trying to sound authoritative.

An arm came up and lazily swiped at her. There was a dull thwack and Adriana was on the ground. As Rafael continued to shamble towards Christine, Adriana rubbed her face then uttered an oath. The other bodies were trembling and starting to moan.

"Get off," Christine cried out as she fought Rafael. For a creature that moments earlier was dead, he was surprisingly strong.

Christine was moving backwards while pushing the thing away. Adriana was struggling to her feet; the hit had caused her to see stars and then she reached up and felt it.

Rafael had Christine up against a wall and his bloodied fingers were clawing at her flesh; his face bent at an odd angle, trying to taste the flesh. "Fucking do something, bitch," she cried out in pain and panic. Her training was out the door. There was nothing that Christine could remember about fighting a foe that was dead and now trying to eat her. Instinctively, she slammed her head into his face.

The undead man stumbled back slightly as it shook its head, which was now at an almost right angle, the vertebrae sticking out of torn skin and dark thick blood oozed out of the wound. Christine smiled to herself triumphantly then quickly brought her arms up.

The metal blade flashed twice, up and down. An unpleasant thwump was followed by blood spurting and hitting the walls then the two arms flopped to the ground. The cuts were clean but bone stumps were left. Adriana spun the blade like a gunfighter. "How was that?"

"He ain't dead yet," Christine exclaimed as the armless being shambled towards her again. With a hard shove from Christine, Rafael spun sharply.

The butcher knife found itself embedded in the cranium of the undead thing. A small moan that sounded more like a sigh came from the slack-jawed face as the eyes rolled up into the sockets and blood dripped down from the wound.

As the body collapsed, Adriana and Christine exchanged worried glances. Quickly, Adriana wrenched the blade free then brought it down another two times until she was satisfied that Rafael would never get back up. "Now," she said happily, "how about some food?"

#

"What the fuck is happening?" Christine gasped once they were outside Papa's. She was bent over and having trouble breathing. Adriana, on the other hand, was calm, cool, and collected. Her eyes were darting from the building filled with moaning to the street. She was hoping that nobody was about to witness this.

"Adriana?"

"Something out of a bad movie," Adriana said with a small chuckle. She had no idea what to make of the attack.

Christine shook her head. "I've been seeing odd things all over. On the radio earlier, I heard that—"

"Not here," Adriana shushed her as she spotted a street food vendor. "Wait here."

#

The Cubano sandwich is one of the greatest pieces of food to ever come out of the Caribbean. Nearly everyone who has one can never have a sandwich, grilled or otherwise, without comparing it to this. This grilled piece of heaven is found all over the world, usually named Cubano, though in Mexico it is called Torta Cubano, which is still the same thing. Every restaurant and street vendor in Havana sells it and is well worth the money. Christine and Adriana watched the chef construct the sandwich while they sipped colas.

On top of a slice of pan Cubano, smear yellow mustard then add slices of ham, mojo pork, cheese, and pickles. Then on another slice, smear more yellow mustard, put together and paint the top slice with melted butter. After all this, you can use either a sandwich press or a grill. On the grill, place the sandwich and then using a cast-iron pan press down. Flip after the cheese has started to melt. The cheese had started to melt when the chef quickly flipped the sandwich. The top was now on the grill and sizzling nicely. The women watched, licking their lips, as the chef took the now perfectly grilled sandwich, slice it diagonally then smacked it down onto a plate. He handed it to them with a nod.

"Gracias," said Christine as she handed a plate to Adriana, "pero un order de yucca fries. Por favor."

The chef nodded and set to work making the yucca fries, the second best food in Cuba. As he did, the two spies sat on a bench and watched the scene across the road.

What had happened was that after they had placed their order, Adriana had gotten onto the policia, leaving a message saying there had been a murder at Papa's and that one of the victims was the concierge of the Nacional. It hadn't taken long for the policia, ambulancia, and other officials to arrive on the scene.

Then something odd happened. The Policia went in and almost immediately they came running out. They were jibbering to the other officials about the undead and now the Army was there.

"I love watching the circus," Adriana said as she took a bite of the sandwich. Christine nodded as she chewed. "A bit of entertainment while we eat; good for the digestion." Adriana laughed at her own joke.

They watched as the coroners waited patiently for the Policia and Army to finish their fight. Christine was solemn as she ate, her eyes and ears on the two most senior men screaming at each other. The coronel was mouthing off about national security and that there was only one way to take care of the situation. The capitan of policia argued that since there was no interest to national security that he was in charge. The coronel then gave him a walkie-talkie with instructions. The chef waddled over with the yucca fries, dropped them on the bench between them. Adriana handed him some pesos then watched as the he waddled back to his kitchen.

"Continue the story," Christine said after a prolonged silence.

Adriana blinked then stared at the restaurant. "Well, there isn't much else to tell. After searching around the Bay and coming up empty, I was heading back to the entrance to get out without any problems. But, you know how problems and trouble follow me around." Christine nodded slightly. Adriana smiled at that then continued, "Those two big bastardos, the Danny Trejo look-alikes, they had been following me and they cornered me. 'Stay away from the Bay,' one said. I laughed; these must be rocket scientists. They continued in this way, warning me about the Bay, that Sanderson was going to be killed no matter what."

"Were they American?" Christine asked. She was looking intently at Adriana.

"No. They were Cubans, from the south, I think. Why?"

Christine didn't say a word, but her eyes moved away from looking at her partner to the restaurant. "Chris," Adriana asked.

"The USA has a policy of not employing any Cuban Nationals at Guantanamo. It's a security reason. They are afraid that with all the renditions happening that one day a prisoner would be Russian. Which would mean that a Cuban employee would be tempted to release or at least help them... Don't look at me like that! They still think of Cuba as being Communist."

"Pendejos," Adriana spat. "They come here and speak about re-establishing talks and dismantling the embargo and yet they all believe we are like Castro! So, these two goons were warning me and trying to generally intimidate me. Which, after a while gets boring. Foreplay is fun and all, but sooner or later, I need to get down to the fucking. So," she grinned, "I kicked one in the huevos. Went down faster than a Cubano does. His amigo looked confused, which gave me enough time to flip him over then follow with a face stomp. Shattered his nose perfectly. While I was wiping the blood off of my shoe, the first one got to his feet. He growled something which made me laugh. I suppose that made him angry because he grabbed me in a bear hug. Which was nice, his muscles felt nice and yes, I got a little wet. Don't give me that look, Chris, you know how much I love to be held."

Christine shook her head as she gulped down the cola. Her hand reached for the yuccas and she bit into one. Delicioso.

"He was grunting and in any other circumstance, I would have been delighted by the noises. Not then though. Too many chances of US troops rounding the corner."

"What did you do?" Christine asked, bored now by the story.

Lacking any interest in what was happening at Papa's, both women failed to notice the Army drenching the building with gasoline. The ambulancia, policia, and coroner all had left the area quietly and the only interested parties were the chef and some stray animals. Four commandos with heavy backpacks stepped up along the perimeter of the building. They were handed a hose which they connected building flamethrowers.

The flames leapt from the barrels and arced high into the night sky. The moment the heat touched the gasoline-covered wood, the building exploded with fire. The heat was so much that every man had to step back, shielding their eyes. From inside, the wood crackled and popped. Then came the moans which soon were small screams and whimpers. The air was filled with the scents of burning wood, melting plastic, and that special smell of burning flesh that people mistake for pork.

After watching the burning building, the coronel gestured and soon the area was clear of any military presence.

"I screamed. As loud as I could," Adriana said with pride. "It didn't take long for the cavalry to appear. They arrested the men and then escorted me out. I saw my contact and was able to convince him to have lunch with me. Long story short... Hey! Where you going?"

#

Christine had stood and was walking across the small road. Adriana ran and quickly caught up with her.

"Que pasa?"

"Your two friends," Christine said with a curt nod of the head. Adriana followed her gaze and her mouth fell open.

"I don't believe it," she whispered as they made their way towards an alley. Hiding in the shadows were two hulking shapes.

"Let's find out what's going on."

Adriana nodded, slightly unnerved now. Christine barely noticed. "What?"

"Nothing."

Christine nodded and waved at the two men.

"Wow," she said. "You two are huge! I mean, I like them big but you! Ah-ma-zing!" She blinked brightly then giggled. The two men looked at each other then at her. Adriana was behind the corner of the wall, waiting for a signal.

"Go away, little girl," the one with a bandage over his nose growled.

"Oh don't be silly!" Christine giggled again and she touched the bigger-than-her head arm affectionately. "I'm from LA, you know, and I need a couple of big dangerous types like yourselves for a photo shoot. What do you say? It pays well and you get to keep the clothes… Whatever happened to your nose?"

"Nada," Bandage growled again as he roughly brushed her hand away.

"You need to go now, little girl," the second one said. He had a slick new haircut and a small beard which did not suit him.

Christine turned to him slowly. "Honey," she began, "firstly, I'm not a little girl. Second, you really should shave off the pubic hair. Make yourself look older and not so… oh I don't know, Christian Priesty."

Bandage laughed, big loud guffaws. "I keep telling him the same thing!"

Slick Cut glared at his brother then turned to Christine. He bent low so he was at her eye level. "You need to leave. Now! Or else I'm going to eat you."

Christine yawned, looking bored. "Pish, I thought you two would be fun. Oh well." She looked downtrodden. "I guess my friend and I should look somewhere else. Darling!"

The two thugs' eyes bulged as Adriana stepped around the

corner. "Yes, my sweet? Oh! You found them!"

"Get her," Bandage snarled.

Christine was quick. She grabbed a trashcan lid and Frisbee'd it into Bandage's gut. As the giant doubled over, his face met with a knee. The nose crunched and collapsed even more. The man screamed.

Adriana ran at Slick Cut who was fumbling with a small Walther PPK handgun. "No you don't," she said then with three swift moves, she had disarmed the man. He threw three high punches at her, the last one connecting with her solar plexus.

Bandage, through teared up eyes, was wrestling with Christine. She was trying to scratch the face. The man laughed as he used his weight to hold her down. Two large slabs of meat wrapped themselves around her small throat and the thug started to squeeze.

Slick Cut picked up Adriana and slammed her into the ground. She grunted as the air escaped her. She tried to crawl away, but her leg was grabbed. As she was dragged back into the fray, Adriana kicked out at the face. Her foot connected with the eye socket and there was a sickening crack followed by a pop and blood. The thug screamed like a goat, clutching at his face.

Adriana got to her feet and rubbed her chest. At least one rib broken, maybe more cracked. A kick into the stomach forced the man onto his back. With grim determination, she picked up the gun. "Todos los Cubanos deberían disparar."

"Nononono no! Por favor," Slick cut begged as Adriana placed the barrel of the gun against his forehead.

"Y disparar bien," she said as her finger squeezed the trigger.

The gunshot echoed louder than a bomb blast through the alley. The face sagged, eyes rolling up as blood oozed from the new orifice. The mouth hung open slackly and the body slumped into a sitting position. Christine and Bandage stopped their struggle and looked up.

Bandage screamed when Adriana kicked the body over. The face stared at the brother, eyes never blinking again. An arm outstretched as if to say "Help me." Adriana squeezed another round into the chest. The dead man flinched from the impact.

"Leave him alone," Bandage howled then made a run for

Adriana. He stopped dead in his tracks when she pointed the firearm at his face.

"Sit down."

The man obeyed, obedient as a dog. Christine struggled to her feet, coughing and rubbing her neck. There would most likely be a bruise from this. *Damn*! She stumbled over to the two. Adriana held the gun an inch from the thug's face.

"Damn, Adriana! That was uncalled for."

Adriana shook her head, a short sharp movement. "We need only one alive. This gorilla seems the more intelligent." She gestured with the gun and the thug started sobbing. "Stop that," she commanded.

The man yelped as the gun slapped his face, causing a small cut to form along his cheek. The bandage on his nose was seeping with fresh blood and there was bone matter sticking out of it. His eyes flashed with anger and his fists curled into balls.

"This is what's going to happen," Christine said. "I'm going to ask you two questions. Answer them both and you'll be free to go and bury your brother. If not, then..." She nodded to Adriana who pressed the gun into the skin of his cheek.

"Fine," Bandage said sullenly.

"Excellent," Christine said happily. "First question, what were you doing at Guantanamo bay?"

"Trying to get this puta," the man nodded at Adriana, "before she ruined everything."

Christine looked at Adriana who shook her head and shrugged her shoulders. Slowly, Christine turned back to the man on his knees; they were covered in blood as a small pool had formed. "Go on."

Bandage chuckled. "Of course, there are no nukes on Cuba! That's the stupidest thing in the world. More-so than Justin Bieber. If she found out and reported back to her bosses about this, then Sanderson would have nothing to worry about and the plan would fail."

"What plan?" Christine whispered. Her mind was working overtime, putting everything together. There were still pieces missing but a picture had started to form.

"Is that the second question?" A look of victory had crept over

Bandage's face.

"Answer her," Adriana said with a quick slap.

He recovered then rubbed his cheek. "Pendeja!"

"Enough of that," Christine barked. "What's the plan? What is Jeremiah Banks up to?"

Another laugh erupted from the giant, it was a barking laugh, the same as a big dog. "Jeremiah Banks is nothing more than a name used by many to scare the government. He hasn't been seen here in years. Not since he publicly humiliated some agent. Now, where was he from? Not FBI. Or CIA. MI6 maybe." The thug was having fun drawing out the conversation. "That's it! The Station. Some perra agent he set up when she got too close to his operation. Had her give up her entire network. Messy business from memory."

Christine kicked the man hard in the chest, sending him backwards. He laughed as he fell then just as quickly stopped when he landed on the dead body of his brother. Christine stood over him then stomped his right ankle. It cracked with a splintering and the bone ripped through the skin. A howl escaped from the thug's mouth.

Adriana stood over him, pointing the gun. "Hush now."

"Where is he?" Christine asked casually.

"No idea," Bandage replied. "Last I heard, he died from some rare disease in Asia. Got it from some whore most likely. Now we all use it. Some for the money and reputation. Others for the power."

"And yourself?"

"Because I can," he answered with a roar of laughter.

Christine turned to Adriana. "Fuck this."

Adriana nodded and pressed the gun into the man's leg. The flesh muffled the sound and all that could be heard was a small POP followed by a moan. He reached for the wound but Adriana swatted the hand away. Christine knelt next to him, making sure to keep herself above the blood.

"Why don't you try to be more polite?"

"Suck my cock!"

Christine shook her head, then slowly she took out a penknife. She opened the blade and with deliberate slowness inserted the tip into the new hole. A little force exerted and the knife easily cut into muscle. "Call me suspicious," she said, "but I don't believe you. Tell me the truth. Who are you working for?"

Bandages clamped his mouth shut and smiled defiantly. Instead of getting mad, Christine shrugged and twisted the knife, causing the blade to open the wound further. She also forced the blade further into the leg. "You can tell me. We're all friends now."

The giant shook his head, biting down on his lip to keep from crying out. Christine continued to wiggle the blade downward until she felt something hard. Bone. She scrapped the blade across it and she could tell that Bandages was in true pain. "Speak up now," she said with a final scrap.

"Jeremiah Banks," the goon screamed. "It's all him! Now please for the love of God stop!" He was sweating and had turned pale. Christine nodded and removed the blade, blood oozed then squirted out of the wound. The blood began to seep and spurt out quicker and quicker.

Adriana tapped Christine's shoulder. "I think you hit an artery" she whispered. Christine shrugged then turned back to the man.

"Tell me more, tell me more."

Bandages was panting now. "He wants the USA to back away from Cuba, leave it alone. He has people all over and every contingency planned for! Ask your—"

The right eye bulged then swiveled to the right as the rest of that side of the face went slack. A small red hole exploded under the eye socket. Blood started to drip out of it. Christine recoiled quickly as three more small holes said hello with little squirts of blood that then started to ooze. She whirled around to see Adriana wipe the weapon down then plant it on the other body.

"I need a shower," she said in reply to Christine's questioning look.

CHAPTER FIFTEEN

Christine stood naked in the bathroom. Her hand wiped the fogged up mirror and she grimaced at the reflection. A large ugly bruise had started to form around her neck from where the giant thug had been strangling her. Her mouth felt scratchy and she knew instantly that for the next day or so her voice would be barely useful. The scratches on her arm stung but were nothing to worry about. Silently, Christine cursed Station Master, Juan de Dios, Adriana, and herself for everything that had happened. *Once upon a time*, she thought, *in a fight there would be no way she would have gotten this injured.*

"You okay," Adriana called through the door.

"Bueno," Christine replied as she stepped into the shower.

It hadn't taken them long to get back to the Nacional. Christine and Adriana had easily avoided the policia after checking the alley for any clues that might lead to them. Then while Adriana kept a lookout, Christine had gone through the pockets of both men. Bandages had nothing of importance on him save for some pesos and a picture of Adriana. It was most likely given to them so they could keep an eye on her. The other one was more inclined to help; his pockets held a wad of money (USA currency), another photo of Adriana, and a hand-written note. It wasn't in Español, but what appeared to be a mixture of Hungarian, French, and Arabic. Whoever had written it had already established this code system with the brothers.

The hotel staff didn't know about Rafael's demise and if they did, they hid their sorrow well.

Adriana was the first to hop into the shower when they entered the room. While she cleaned herself, Christine sat at a table, positioned in front of one of the windows, and stared out at the sea. She didn't know what the time was, but it had to be late. The moon was full and its light bathed all of Havana in a gentle glow. The waves reflected it and some of the stars. It was truly beautiful and helped Christine put her thoughts in order.

The first thing she did was pick up the phone and rang the Buena Vista Social Club. When the woman answered, she asked for Juan. It took a minute until she heard the sigh followed by, "This better be good."

"You've been fucking me from minute one," was her opener as she had limited time before Adriana finished. That meant she had no time to be polite.

"Christine? What's happened?" He sounded surprised and concerned. Apparently, he had forgotten their conversation earlier.

"Yeah, it's me," she said. "I've just been attacked by a couple of Jeremiah Banks' goons. That's right, he is back! Oh and also a goddamn zombie! So what the fuck is going on with you?"

Juan didn't say a word for what seemed like an eternity. Christine kept one ear to the shower; the moment she heard it switch off she would need to hang up, act all nonchalant. She heard the breathing on the other end as Juan tried to figure out what was going on.

Finally, "Christine, I don't know what happened tonight. We've been busy trying to see if our network of informants has been burned. Rafael Cienfuentes has been murdered."

"I know! I made the call. Not before he tried to eat my face… This proves he's back."

"Christine, my dear, this doesn't prove anything. Rafael had gambling debts. Chances are, he was killed over a bad check…"

"Bullshit! There is no Shylock in the world that would massacre an entire restaurant to get one deadbeat."

Juan sighed. "We can never know what someone is capable of doing, Christine, until they actually do it."

"How philosophical. There were two giant goons that attacked us. We were able to question one and he gave up Banks. Definitely him that is behind the threats. There! Bring him in, Juan."

"Pinche…" Juan stopped himself. "I need proof. Can you get these men to talk to me?"

"No," Christine said softly. "We had to kill them."

There was a long pause. "Who is we? Are you working with someone?"

"Of course I am," Christine said, exasperation washing over her. "Station Master put me in contact with one of your agents. They've been helping me. A lot more than you have old man."

"Who?" Juan asked, his voice sounded worried. "Who are you working with?"

"If you don't know, how can you help me?"

"…What do you mean a zombie?"

Christine nearly threw the phone across the room. *What the fuck is happening to the world*? "I tried asking you earlier and you ignored me. Now, now! You want to know? Fine. I have seen it, so don't think I'm lying to you. I have seen the dead get back up and try to eat me. There are fucking zombies in Cuba!" She laughed at that last statement.

"Christine, are you positive that they were dead?"

"Oh for fuck sake… Yes, Juan, I am positive. Seven shots, point blank to the chest does that. Maybe this has something to do with the State of Emergency?"

She couldn't hear anything except the shower, which was good, she hoped. Juan better have something otherwise the whole situation was fucked and her instincts were screaming to get the hell out of Dodge.

"That would explain the mess," he said slowly. His tone was deadly and Christine knew something else had happened.

"What happened, Juan?"

"Those two men you say you killed? They weren't."

"What? No fucking way!"

"They killed five of the police that showed up. All had to be burned… Christine, maybe you should seriously consider leaving Cuba? Go back to the Station. Or better yet, get out of the business."

"No," she said quietly. "Juan, what do you think about the dead rising? Could it be true?"

Juan de Dios laughed; it was devoid of any humor. "Not

without the help of evil. My family came from Haiti originally and the only religion I know is Voodoo."

"¿En serio?"

"Si," he said. "But not what Hollywood says. In Voodoo, zombies are not the undead, but bodies that are forcibly used, against their will, to do the bidding of one person. The idea of the dead rising? That is something that Hollywood and bad writers have used. There is no way for that to happen, Christine..."

"Then what could be causing the sickness and what has been happening?"

Before the old spy master could answer, Christine slammed the phone back onto its receiver. Adriana had exited the shower and was now standing the doorway to the bedroom. She had a towel wrapped around her body. It hugged her, accentuating her curves and leaving little to the imagination. Her hair was wet and plastered to her face and neck. "That was refreshing! You should have one, Chris. Wash all your troubles away."

Christine nodded and headed into the bathroom, cursing her terrible luck.

She tilted her head back, letting the water wash her. It felt good, the pressure from each drop of water hitting her skin. The little pinpricks kept her mind focus, which was what she needed right now. As she washed her hair, she started to make a list of everything she knew to be true.

Jeremiah Banks was indeed in charge of the plot to kill President Sanderson. No man under the torture she had dealt out would lie, would he? That was the first fact. Juan de Dios was hiding something, which wasn't odd since all spy masters do that. But since he had seen her that first time at Buena Vista, his interactions with her had seemed forced. Almost as if he didn't want to be around her for some reason. Both Adriana and Juan had never mentioned each other; did they actually work together? Christine would ask both at some point, probably after the case. She only had two more days left until the end of the festival and nothing much to show for it. Just a certainty about Jeremiah Banks and the note.

"Chris, you mind if I pour us some drinks?" Adriana called through the door.

"Go for it."

Why would Station Master use Adriana as the contact after all they had been through? That was the most perplexing question she had at the moment. *Time to get some damn answers*, she thought.

Christine turned off the shower and wrapped a towel around her.

#

She grabbed another towel and put her hair up. Christine had always hated the feeling of wet hair on her neck and face and thought anyone who did was barbaric. So when she entered the main room and saw Adriana lounging on one of the couches with her hair all over the back of it, Christine was struck with a moment of disgust. "Do something with your hair."

Adriana smiled and held up a glass of rum. In a highball. No mixer. Just the pure rum. The glass was half full and glistened with condensation. "Drink up," Adriana said, handing Christine the glass.

Christine sipped the rum, savoring the flavors as it washed down her throat. "Your hair," she said, "get it off the couch please."

The Cuban giggled, downed the rest of her rum, looked around for a towel then realizing that there was nothing else she shrugged and took her towel off of her body then wrapped her head. Christine tried not to stare, but the Cuban's body was alluring; voluptuous in all the right ways and darker than most other Cubans Christine had seen. There was a slight speckling of freckles over the heavy breasts that came from years of sunbathing.

"Are you drunk?" Christine asked tersely as she sat on the couch opposite Adriana. Christine's eyes started to wander and she had to force herself to look elsewhere.

Adriana sat with her legs slightly apart, her eyes twinkling, and she smiled. "Not borracha pero mellow," she giggled and poured herself another.

Christine shook her head as she sipped the rum. "Some night, huh?"

"Dios mio! I haven't had this much fun in years... Come to think of it, not since you left," Adriana said as she stared at the amber liquid.

"Yeah," Christine agreed, "me too. It felt good being in the field getting into trouble with you again... What do you think of Rafael?" She waited, watching Adriana's face, waiting for the reaction.

"Probably wasn't fully dead yet."

"And how do you explain the continuous movement after losing his arms?"

Adriana blinked then rubbed her face. "Running on adrenaline... or something stronger."

"Aye por favor," Christine sighed. "Give me a fucking break. Can't you see what is happening? Even Juan knows."

The Cuban sitting opposite her stared at the bottle. "Adriana?"

A sigh escaped from the full lips. "There is no such thing as a zombie," she said. "We were told stories about the dead rising from the grave. Not because of magic, or any such thing... Forget about it." Adriana turned her head, embarrassed by what she was about to say.

Christine nudged the table with her foot; the noise startled Adriana. "Go on. This is a safe space." She watched as the Cuban picked up the bottle of rum. Her eyes focused on the liquid as it moved inside the bottle. Adriana's eyes were completely fixated on the amber beverage, as if she was hypnotized.

"The only way for the dead to come back," she finally said, "is not from magic, or science or demons. But...from the sins of man. When the Lord is fed up with man's wicked ways, he... Que paso?"

Christine had a slightly amused look on her face. "No, please go on."

Adriana shook her head. "You think I'm a silly superstitious peasant. Pinche pendeja!"

"Fuck you very much. Just finish what you were saying, por favor?" She watched as Adriana took a swig from the bottle.

"Well, before the Rapture, he will start judgment by sending a plague to wipe out the sinners. The undead. Those who have been found guilty have been given the purpose of bringing us all for judgment... That's all."

"So," Christine started, "if we have forgiveness, then the

undead will leave us alone?"

A slow long nod from Adriana. "Forgiveness is all we have these days."

Christine laughed as she looked at her own glass. "Don't think I've forgiven you. Bitch," she said as she took a long gulp of her rum.

"Por favor!" Adriana pleaded "I did my nacional duty."

"National duty! Please, you were working for Jeremiah Banks. Do you know what that did to me? My reputation at the Station? Fuck you." Christine finished the drink, grabbed the bottle, and filled her glass. "Have you ever been honest?"

Adriana looked hurt for a microsecond. "Everyday with you I was. For some reason, I can't lie to you."

"Bullshit! You're a spy, you lie for a living. Pendeja." Christine took another drink and as she wriggled to get comfortable, her towel became loose and slipped down her chest, exposing her bosom and the scar.

"What the hell is that?" Adriana pointed at the scar.

"The fuck you care for? This is what happened after you fucked me over."

Christine ran a finger along the scar and her face clouded over with painful memories. Adriana got up, went over, and knelt before her. Her face was full of remorse. "How did that happen?"

"After you sold my team out and they were all killed. Did I thank you for that?" Christine didn't wait for an answer. "You know they never found the bodies. I suppose Jeremiah Banks had them buried or at least anchored and dumped into the bay. Well, after all that, I had to make contact with Station Master. The old man tore me apart, and he put out a burn notice."

"He did that?"

Christine nodded slowly. "I didn't know at the time. It wasn't until I went to Juan for help that I knew I had been burnt. He wasn't happy to see me, which was rare for the man. Always treated me like family. That day he looked like the grim reaper. Told me he was sorry and that there was nothing he could do. Next thing I remember is being black bagged."

"Puta madre!"

"Your shock helps my pain. When I could see next, they had

me strapped into a chair and an ancient Cuban was asking all sorts of questions. This man must've been around during the Batista regime."

"Short? Mustache? Big mole on one eyelid?"

Christine nodded.

Adriana shook her head, impressed. "That was Santiago Durán, the top interrogator in all of Cuba. For him to come out of retirement to work on you... Juan must've really wanted to know all your secrets."

"Well, if I ever get to see him again, I'll make sure to say Hola properly."

"He died a couple of years ago, Chris."

Christine punched the couch hard. "Another thing to cross off the bucket list then. Fuck me!"

Adriana reached out a tentative finger and began to trace the shape of the scar. "How did they do this?"

"He didn't. I don't know how long I was there for, but he kept asking two questions. Where is Jeremiah Banks and why would The Station burn me..." Christine stopped talking. Her eyes met Adriana's who smiled. Slowly, Christine raised a hand, laid it on top of Adriana's and then removed it. "Do you know the worst thing about torture?" Adriana shook her head. "Of course you wouldn't. You never felt real pain. The worst thing is not the pain or the devices used. It is the knowledge that sooner or later you'll talk. Eventually, you run out of stories to tell. Doesn't matter how good a liar you are. At some point, you will have nothing else to say except for what they want. That's what happened. I spilled everything I knew. The old man just nodded and recorded everything."

"Chris... You can't beat yourself up about it. Anyone would have caved too."

"I don't blame me," Christine said softly. "I blame you. You have been both the best and worst thing to ever happen to me. At some point, Juan paid me a visit, told me about the burn notice and that I had to escape. The order had come down that I was to be killed, executed as a foreign terrorist. Courtesy of the Cuban Government and Station Master. But Juan didn't like that. He had a plan. 'Unfortunately,' he said, 'it is going to hurt a lot.' Then he shot me. Point blank with a .9mm. What you see is the result of the operations. Five in total."

Adriana sat on the floor, looking up at the other woman. She couldn't believe what she had just been told. "Chris, I'm... por favor forgive me!"

Christine Moore stared at her former lover. "Why should I," she asked. "Since arriving here, you and Juan have not been straight with me at all. Don't! How the hell do I know this isn't another setup? Not once has either of you two mentioned the other or that you work together. Don't you dare feed me the line about working in different sections. CI isn't big enough to need more than one team. So, what the hell is going on?"

The Cuban's big brown eyes stared up at the ceiling. Her breathing was slow and rhythmic. Christine's own eyes traced the body before her and memories full of pleasure danced through her mind. "Do you remember that trip we took to Trinidad?"

"When we both had to be the honey-pot? For the Germans." Christine nodded.

"That was the first time we shared a bed. The night before we met the Germans, I told you all about my life. My family. You listened and said what?"

"I said that the past is the past. We shouldn't be chained to it."

Adriana nodded. "You should listen to your own advice. Does it matter whether or not Juan and I speak about each other? No. Por que? We have a job to do. Stop a plot that could destroy Cuba. That is what is at stake here. Not the world. Not the pinche USA. But Cuba. My country. Your haven. So stop being childish, Christine."

"That's rich coming from you."

Adriana snorted. "If you think we're keeping things from you, welcome to the world of spies! You were a traitor to your organization. Is it any wonder we are a little quiet around you?"

Christine stood then grabbed Adriana by the hair and pulled the Cuban to her feet. "Listen to me, you tight twot! The only reason they branded me that was because of you! I get professional courtesy and all. But for fuck sake, I was here for five years!"

Adriana slapped the hands away and backed up. "It's not my fault you couldn't control your tongue and pussy. Five years is a long time and for all I knew you were going to fuck me over at some point."

"Get the fuck out."

Adriana blinked, "What?"

"You heard me. Get out."

The Cuban chuckled. "Same old Christine. Work gets tough and you just power through it. Private life hits a bump and you tell it to hit the road."

"Tell me something honest then."

Adriana shook her head. "Besame primero."

Christine laughed. "Why? Can't get anyone else?"

"Fine." Adriana turned and went into the bedroom.

Christine stood there, thinking about everything they had just talked about then as Adriana returned, clothed and at the door, Christine took four long strides, spun the Cuban around, and kissed her.

"Jeremiah Banks has something really special planned for tomorrow. The tour at the cigar factory. Intel says it will bring the house down."

"Not good enough," Christine breathed then kissed her again.

Adriana breathed deeply then sighed after the kiss. "Presidente Esposito doesn't want the talks to happen."

Christine took a step back. Adriana grabbed her arm. "Why? What's he afraid of?" Christine muttered.

"The same thing as all Cuban presidentes: The return to the old ways. Cuba being another Puerto Rico. The typical bullshit."

Christine shook her head. "No. No. There's something here we're missing. I can feel it." She turned around and went back to the couch and sat deep in thought.

"What just happened?" Adriana asked as she took the seat opposite Christine.

"The USA is not the superpower it once was. The only way for Cuba to become another territory is if Sanderson offered something Cuba can't get on its own. But what?"

Adriana stretched. "Democracy. Financial security. Who knows or cares?"

"Don't do that. You know I hate it when you answer a question with a question." Adriana chuckled but Christine ignored her. "What would happen if Cuba told the USA to go fuck itself?"

"The embargo stays up, probably gets tougher. Cuba gets drained of its resources, goes into a major recession and then…"

Both ladies jumped to their feet and spoke at the same time, "The USA would come riding in as a hero!"

"That's the plan! Sanderson is going to say or do something so offensive that Esposito is forced to decline any offer made. Then Sanderson has every right to turn round and bitch slap Cuba. Give it three years or so and when Cuba is at its weakest come back as the savior of a nation and get what? What resources does Cuba have that the USA needs?"

Adriana was standing next to Christine with her arms wrapped around the blonde's mid-section. "Land. Cuba has the best soil for growing crops. The USA needs unsullied land for the farmers."

"Makes sense," Christine crowed excitedly. "So then if Sanderson is killed… No, that would result in a war; Jeremiah Banks won't want that. Too much at risk… If there was a credible threat to the president, one that would make him flee that would mean Esposito wouldn't have to say no to any agreement. Right?"

"Maybe, but the WMDs are just too obvious. It would have to be something believable."

Christine nodded as they both started to sway, their hips moving as one. She let out a soft moan as Adriana caressed her neck. "That's nice."

"I missed this."

Christine nodded, her eyes closed slightly, "Assassination is good. But there has to be proof… What if the factory tour is just a setup? There will be traces of an assassin. A gun or tripod. Maps. Things like that… You don't think Esposito has Juan talking to Jeremiah Banks about all this? The government working with a known…"

Adriana spun Christine and kissed her. It was passionate with a promise of ecstasy to come later. They both moaned.

"Shut up, missy," Adriana said before planting another kiss full of fuego on Christine's soft, moist lips.

CHAPTER SIXTEEN

The sun was warm as it hit Christine's face. The slit between the heavy curtains allowed just enough light to seep in and bathe her in its warm glow. She smiled and shifted slightly trying to escape the day. Christine rolled over and reached out. Her arm touched nothing, just the linen sheets. Slowly, her eyes opened. "Adriana?"

There was no answer. Christine sat up and rubbed her chest. She stretched slowly, looking around. "Adriana?"

She waited, listening for the shower or movement in the kitchen. Getting to her feet, Christine wrapped a robe around herself. She tied it tightly then went into the main room.

There was no one else in the suite. The curtains had been drawn, the windows opened, and the place had been tidied. Christine rubbed her head, looking around, trying to remember what they had done the night before. She saw the ashtray full of cigar nubs and three empty bottles of rum. They had had a party. There were cushions strewn across the room and some of the chairs had been upturned.

Christine grabbed a bottle of water and went to one of the balconies.

Outside, it was beautiful, not a cloud in the sky. The sea was a clear crystal blue. People were surfing and there were the fishing boats peppered across it.

Christine took a deep breath, held it as her mind traced the previous night. They had made love, that much she could remember. But why? Deep in her heart, Christine knew she still couldn't trust Adriana one hundred percent. *So why the intimacy?* she thought. What had they discovered?

Rafael's body flashed into her mind. Christine released the breath and took a long drink of water. It felt good. Her mind started to clear. They had found him then fought with the twins and had come back to get clean. She had spoken to Juan and they fought. Then she fought with Adriana. *Damn*, Christine thought, *why the fuck am I fighting the only people who can help?*

"Because you are an idiot," she said to herself.

She looked down at the traffic. The Malecón was empty; no cars, no people, and no bands. Absolutely nothing. Christine scratched her head. This was odd. She felt a tugging from the back of her head, like there was something important she had to do.

Christine reached into her robe pocket and pulled out the piece of paper that she had gotten off of Slick Cut. She unfolded it and stared at the writing. It still didn't make sense. What did this have to do with the plot... The plot! She smiled to herself as it all came back.

The WMDs were a ruse to throw all the agencies off the trail of the real plot to setup a fake assassination attempt so that the gringos would leave the country before the end of the festival, thus stopping any of the talks between the USA and Cuba. It all started to make sense now. Finally, Christine felt ahead of the curve.

She went over to the desktop humidor that had been delivered and opened it. It was full of cigars, matches, and a cutter. She reached inside and pulled out the satellite phone. She dialed quickly as she untied the robe.

"Agent Moore here. Connect me to the Signal Box."

She waited as the tell-tale click of the secure line becoming engaged sounded, followed by slight static. Why they didn't upgrade the secure lines she had no idea. Sometimes it was a pain.

"You bitch," Signal's voice echoed slightly.

"Nice to hear your voice, too."

Signal laughed. "You go to Cuba without saying bye? I have to hear it from the Old Man himself!"

"Awww did I hurt your feelings?" Christine asked as she started to pace the room.

"Fuck you." Signal's voice was light. Christine had never met her face to face; that was how Station Master wanted it. It meant no one could be given up easily. "So?" Signal said. "What do you want?"

"I have a note here that needs translating."

"How soon do you need it?"

"Yesterday. I don't know the language, but it looks like a mixture of Hungarian, French, and maybe Arabic."

"Send a pic."

Christine laid the page on the table, flattened it the best she could, and then used the phone to send a photo. "You got it?"

"Hang on." Signal sounded tense for some reason. Christine stared at the page while she waited. The tugging feeling came back. She ignored it.

"The translator is having trouble," Signal said. "It seems like the words are literally made up of thirds of those languages you said. It's going to take some time. Sorry."

"Shit." Christine scrunched the paper into a ball and placed it into the humidor. "Send a text of it the moment it gets done. Okay?"

"Yep yep… So, how's the festival going? Gotten laid?"

Christine laughed. "A lady never kiss and tells."

"True, but whoever said you were a lady?" They both laughed and Christine felt at ease. "So, no juicy gossip?"

"What do you mean? What have you heard?"

"Nothing." Signal went on the defense.

Christine shook her head. "Sorry. I'm running on fumes."

"You okay?"

"Think you…" Christine rubbed her face, her mind fuzzy. "Sig."

"Yeah?"

"Do you," she paused, not sure what to say. "Do you think the dead can come back?"

"Like ghosts or something?"

"Nononono more like…fuck! The more I think about it, the crazier it sounds."

"What the fuck are you on about?"

Christine steeled herself. "There's something seriously fucked up happening in Cuba…"

There was a slight chuckle from Signal. "What else is new?"

"Not like that." Christine was exasperated. "The dead are fucking coming back! Like, and I can't fucking believe I'm fucking saying this, but like zombies!"

There she had said it properly, not only to herself but to the entire world! It felt good. Now she was waiting for the inevitable laughter from Signal. That would be the rational and reasonable reaction to hearing about goddamn fucking zombies.

Instead, Signal said, "Not surprising. Really."

"What?"

"Did I stutter?" Signal asked sarcastically. "It makes sense. With today's modern medicine and technology, it would be quite easy to put an implant in the brain that would affect the motor neurons... Or something like that."

Christine blinked. "You are amazing, Signal!"

"Well, without actually seeing one of these in action, I can't give you a definite answer."

Christine was smiling but as a thought entered her mind, the grin faded. "It couldn't be that."

"Do tell why?"

She sighed. "Whatever is happening is not isolated. It's all over the island. So an implant would have to be done in a medical facility. State of the art. Like something out of science fiction. Fuck!"

She was getting agitated now. Christine wanted to beat the shit out of someone. Anyone. Her hand started to squeeze the plastic-covered phone in her hand.

"Leave it with me, Chris," Signal said. "Now, fucked anyone?"

"I've gotta go, Signal."

"Party pooper."

Christine hung up, placed the phone back in its hiding spot then went to the small kitchenette. She needed some food. A smile formed when she saw the small fruit platter laid out for her. Christine took a fork and started to eat. It was deliciously sweet and juicy. She moaned slightly.

Her eyes noticed an envelope leaning against the kettle. The handwriting was elegant and feminine; Adriana's writing. On the front was one word: Christine.

Slowly, she picked it up and tore the seal open. Then she tipped it upside down and watched as the page slid out and floated to the floor. Using the juice-drenched fork, Christine opened the letter. Her eyes skimmed the lovely writing:

Chris,

Last night was amazing. I'm sorry I had to leave early but duty calls.

A couple of things I didn't get to tell you; your tongue did most of the work.

1) Do not trust Juan. He hasn't been going to the meetings with the CIA and Esposito.

Also, he doesn't seem to care about what is happening with Jeremiah Banks. His attention is only on that bar of his. Do not trust him and try not to be alone with him.

2) The moment you read this, get your fine trasero to the Old Partagas factory. Remember?

I'll see you later, after today's activities. And please try not to kill anyone else, por favor!

Christine smiled as she read the note. She always loved Adriana's handwriting. Her eyes read the part about Juan and she thought, *Yeah that's what he'd say about you too. What are they playing?*

Her eyes grew wide when she read the part about the Old Partagas factory. She glanced to the wall-mounted clock and swore. It was already ten-thirty.

Christine hauled ass to get dressed in comfortable clothes, linen pants and a button-down shirt. She threw on a pair of walking shoes, splashed water on her face and hair then was out the door.

#

Out of all the Cuban cigar brands, there are three that rank among the best for cigar lovers the world over: Cohiba, Montecristo, and Partagas. Each one has its own unique history and vitolas that people love. Cohiba was once just made for Fidel Castro and given as gifts to visiting dignitaries. Then, in the 1990s, it was released to the general public. Montecristo has always been a favorite, but not just because of the relation to the fabled Count. Go to any cigar event and ask people what their favorite Cuban is and most people will say a Montecristo No. 2. The torpedo is one of the perfect sizes to smoke, not too long and not too short.

As for Partagas, it has its own lovers, but one of the biggest draws is the factory. Since 1845 when the first factory was built, the brand has steadily become one of the top selling in the country, second to the Montecristo. The owners have either been murdered on the tobacco plantations, disappeared mysteriously, or have had the factory seized by the government, thanks to Fidel Castro. Since the 1960 Revolution, Partagas was one of the sixteen other factories to have been taken over by Castro's Government and is now controlled by Habanos S.A. In 2012, the factory was moved three kilometers away from Old Havana and the factory has been renamed Francisco Pérez Germán Factory and has become one of the many turista destinations for cigars.

Christine had to fight her way to the factory located on Calle Industria. The traffic was stopped, the detour signs barely registering for the taxis, buses, and people walking the streets. She hoped that nothing had happened to Sanderson. Then she reminded herself to get a full itinerary from Juan; if there was anyone who could give her one it would be him. If not, then she would go to Adriana.

She hadn't taken a taxi and part of her was thankful for that. Even though the taxis were excellent in Havana, riding around in an old Cadillac is fun and all, but when you are in a rush then the best thing to do is walk it. Or run, which is what Christine had done. She had run along the Malecón until she came to Calle Galiano then turned right. There were more people and cars here. "Fuck me!"

Pushing through the crowd, she eventually made it to the intersection of Galiano and Neptuno. Continuing to push through the unwashed masses, she then turned again to the right onto Industria and scolded herself for sleeping in. It was packed with people, buses, reporters, news vans, and the CIA. Everyone was walking one step at a time and she had to remind herself to be polite as she moved through the throng.

Some of the people were Cuban and they gladly let her pass. The turistas, on the other hand, wouldn't give her the time of day, unless they were asking for a date.

At last, she saw the factory. It was old and grand. There had been some renovations done to it over the years, and it had the appearance of an old woman trying to look young. But here it succeeded.

A part of Christine couldn't wait to get in. For the entire time she had been stationed in Havana, she had never had the time to visit it and had always regretted it. Now was her chance. Hopefully.

Next to the factory is an equally old La Casa de Habanos, the official shop for all Habanos sold in Cuba. You can find them in most countries around the world except for the USA. There was the regular crowd standing in front of it, aficionados and the people newly initiated into the world of cigars. Also standing around were the locals selling cigars for a huge discount. They would say they got them from an amigo in the factory. Nine times out of ten, the cigar was a fake made with the floor sweepings from the factories. Inside, though, one could find the best cigars available, or so Christine used to think. She shook her head as she watched a young man hand over two hundred Cuban pesos to one of the scalpers then walk away like he had found the holy grail. She turned her attention back to the factory.

In front of it, a small podium had been erected. The CIA stood guard all around the immediate vicinity. That would be where Sanderson would make his appearance before heading in for a private tour. Christine looked up at the various windows of the factory. *If I was a sniper*, she thought, *where would I position myself?*

The answer didn't matter unless she could get in. How she was going to do that was beyond her.

The crowd started to cheer and push in towards the podium. Standing behind a microphone was President Sanderson, looking completely different to how he had the last time Christine saw him. His hair was neatly combed and parted, face clean shaven, and he smiled beatifically at the mass in front of him. He raised his hands and all went quiet with a hushed awe.

"Thank you all so much for coming out today!" he began. "As most of you know, this was THE crown jewel of all the cigar factories in Havana. But, unfortunately, progress must happen and Partagas was relocated to newer and better accommodations." Sanderson paused and looked up at the old building. "It is indeed beautiful, but has fallen into disrepair... No matter though, because due to some entrepreneurs, this fine building is going to be refurbished and used to produce the first new Cuban cigar brand since the Cohiba was made publicly available. I am happy to be the first to announce the name of the brand... La Perpetua!"

The mass of people cheered and whooped. Christine didn't bother to look around or at the president. She kept her eyes on the old shuttered windows, looking for any sign of movement.

"As many of you know," Sanderson continued, "there are tours of this fine building and before reconstruction begins, I am going to take it AND roll my own vitola. A..." he looked to his left at a gorgeous Cuban in a suit, most likely his handler who leaned towards him and whispered something in his ear "...torpedo!"

A cheer exploded from the mass as Sanderson was ushered into the building by the CIA. Christine watched as he waved and smiled at the cameras. Then he was gone. Quickly, Christine looked around for anyone who might be able to get her in.

"Christine!" Juan shouted to her and waved. He was wearing a light blue suit and was leaning on his cane. "I didn't think you were going to make it. I got word from The Station that you would need entrance."

"Really?" Christine said when she got over to him. "When did you get the message?"

"Early this morning. Believe me, it took some time to arrange it. I don't have the clout I once did. But, here." He handed her a pass that said PRESS.

"Muchisimas gracias!" She hugged him. "Do me a favor and find out everything you can about La Perpetua?"

Juan looked at her oddly. "Why? They have no link to Jeremiah Banks."

"Just do it, por favor!" Christine begged as she turned and sprinted towards the entrance. Juan stood there, looking confused then did what he always did when confused: took a sip from a hip flask and lit up a cigar.

#

Christine whispered a small thanks to Juan. Without the pass, she would have had to break into the building and that would definitely have caused more problems. As it was, she was able to join the small group as it passed the old reception area.

The reporters were wrestling to get close enough to Sanderson to ask him questions, take photos, and record video of the president. Each time one would get close enough, the CIA agents would push them back. This happened three times before the president noticed.

They had come to a stairwell and he went up two steps. Stopped. Then turned around, "You all must have tons of questions. I'm happy to answer one now."

He looked over the small group of people; all had their hands raised as is the protocol. He ignored the men and focused on the women. Christine stood in the back, hiding from his view but keeping an eye on everyone. She could tell that Sanderson was looking for a beautiful lady to speak with, try to impress, woo, then later take her back to his room.

"You there," he said, pointing, "the pretty little red head."

A petite British reporter giggled as she took a step forward. "Thank you, Mister President." Her accent was upper-middle class, probably from London itself. "My question is a little unrelated to today's proceedings."

"Unrelated questions are my favorite," Sanderson said with a megawatt smile.

"Well…then…my question is this. You are the first president to be invited to the Habanos Festival. So far, you have been seen at all of the major events and you do seem to be having a fun time."

"Oh, definitely."

The reporter giggled and played with her hair. "There has been lots of speculation, Mister President, about why you are really here. A new trade agreement? Buying stock in the cigar market? Looking for a new wife?"

"It's a trial separation," Sanderson said with a slight shift in tone. He now spoke like a father scolding a child. "My wife and I are not getting a divorce."

"My apologies, Mister President," the reporter said rather too quickly. She knew she had lost her moment and had to recover. "Well, my question is this… Are the rumors about the talks between Presidente Esposito and yourself regarding Cuba becoming another territory of the United States true?"

Sanderson chuckled dismissively. "See," he said, "this is what happens when you let women ask the serious questions. My dear, you must realize that when two heads of state get together, they have a multitude of issues to discuss. President Esposito and I have had meetings. True…"

Christine trailed off, her mind wandering to the building she was in. Sanderson was just spouting the usual presidential drivel designed to bamboozle reporters. He was a natural at this, which is why Christine was able to move away from the group and make her way up the emergency stairs to the next floor.

The Partagas factory has three floors not including the roof. The factory was small but able to produce as many as ten million cigars per year, almost as much as Montecristo.

On the second floor, Christine could not see anything, just large bulky tables covered by sheets. This must have been where the rolling happened, the Galera. She took a deep breath. All the smells had become ingrained into all the wood surfaces, tobacco and premium Cuban leaf. Christine Moore was in heaven.

"I don't fucking believe this!" The man's voice snapped her out of her reverie.

Don stood next to a small cabinet. He wore a T-shirt and cargo shorts, looking more like a turista than an agent. In one hand, he held the handle of a large carry-case, the heavy-duty kind that are used to transport cameras, valuable technical equipment, and weapons. In the other was a small notebook. The expression he wore was one of absolute disbelief.

"Hola, guapo," Christine said with a smile, noticing the bandage wrapped around his left hand. "What happened? Did some little piggies go to market and forget to come home?" She laughed.

"What the hell are you doing here?" he asked, hefting the case in is hand.

"Oh, I just thought I'd pop by and stop a killer."

Don glanced around the room, hoping for an escape route.

"Why don't you put that down? It looks heavy," Christine said, taking a step forward.

Don shook his head rapidly. "You can't fuck this up for me. Not again. I need this."

"Oh? Do tell."

The man smiled then his eyes flickered to just behind her. Christine turned in time to see Sanderson and the rest start to appear from the stairs.

"Gun! Gun!" Don shouted.

The CIA agents swarmed the area, pushing past Sanderson, going straight for Christine. She grinned sheepishly at them then ran like a bat out of hell.

Don was already on the move, barreling up the stairs onto the next floor. As Christine dodged the tables nearing the cabinet, she grabbed it and pulled. It toppled over, clanging to the ground and spilling its guts. Old torcedores equipment, the chaveta, goma containers, tablas, casquillos, the cepos and guillotinas tumbled out of the cabinet right into the path of the agents. They tripped and skidded. "Leave them!" Sanderson barked as the reporters started taking videos and asking awkward questions.

Christine leapt up the last couple of steps onto the third floor. This was where the cigars were put into boxes and had the bands applied. Stacks of pre-cut wood towered over her. There were far too many places for Don to lay ambush.

A noise caught her attention.

"Come out, come out, wherever you are!"

"Finders keepers," Don called back.

His voice came from near the back. He was close to the stairs to the roof. If she wasn't careful, he might be able to get away. Christine moved slowly down the room. Each step she made as silently as she could. Any movement she heard she spun towards; a mouse here, a cockroach there. She was sweating and trembling.

"Colder. Colder," Don's voice bounced throughout the room. In the distance, she could hear the oncoming storm of the CIA. She would have to do something fast.

"You really are in over your head," Don was saying. "Why not just go back to your hotel and let the inevitable happen?"

"I hate waiting," Christine replied as she gave a hard shove to one of the stacks of wood. It swayed back and forth before collapsing against another stack.

The domino effect was magnificent to watch as each tower of wood fell one after the other. The wave of wood crashed against the stairwell, blocking it.

Christine turned back and saw Don's feet stampeding up the stairs. "Fuck," she said to herself.

#

The carry-case smashed into her stomach the moment Christine emerged into the open. She doubled over, grabbing the handle. She spun to the left and the movement wrenched it away from Don. Christine kicked out at him and he danced backwards. She bent over, breathing hard.

Don didn't wait for her to recover properly. He dived at her, picked the woman up, and then threw her into the wall of the stairs.

Christine collided hard with the wall and was thankful for the support. Don was upon her again, throwing punches at her face. She ducked down and the first hit contacted the wall.

Don winced then recoiled, holding his hand. Christine lashed out with her leg, connecting with his and continuing the follow through. The man fell flat on his ass.

Christine got to her feet and went for the case. She hoped there was a knife or handgun in it. There were questions that needed answering. Her hand found the latch as Don grabbed her leg. He pulled, dragging her across the cement.

"You really are a pain in my ass," he panted, using his free hand to hold Christine's other leg.

He was pulling her towards the edge. Christine looked around, reaching out for any weapon she could find. Then she saw it.

"Glad to be of help," she said through gritted teeth. Then using her own body as leverage she bent upwards. With her arms, she reached up and grabbed Don's hands.

He stopped then turned.

Christine pulled back, using gravity to flip the man.

She watched as he sailed over her then kissed the cement with his face. His momentum kept him going and he slid across the roof, leaving a trail of blood and clumps of flesh.

Christine stood and dusted herself down then started walking towards him. "Rule one, Donny, never claim victory until the battle is over."

"Couldn't agree more," the man growled as he lunged at her with a switchblade.

He sliced down and got her arms which she had brought up in defense. Christine winced and cried out but spun, landing an elbow against his back.

Don grunted but recovered quickly. He turned and drove the blade towards her. Christine brought her hands down to break his wrist. He was expecting this and as she made the move, he turned to the left and spun around her. The blade traced along her back and the blood stained her shirt.

Christine cried out and then grabbed his arm as Don lunged. She pulled while at the same time ducking down and driving her fist into his knee.

Don's own momentum made him fall onto the blade. It slid easily into his stomach as he hit the roof. He rolled and coughed blood. Only the very tip of the hilt was visible.

Christine knelt next to the man. "Confess your sins."

Don tried to laugh. Instead, he coughed up blood and squealed like a pig. Christine looked at the wound and knew one thing. He would be dead soon.

"Now is the time to confess," she said. "Unburden yourself and find peace."

The dying man shook his head. "No point."

He was wheezing and his breathing was weak. He had turned pale and there was so much blood leaking from the wound. *The fall must have torn open the cut*, Christine thought.

"There always is."

Again, he shook his head. "We are all damned if we do and damned if we don't... That's what happens...when...yo...you work for the...devil."

His eyes closed and his head lolled to the side. Christine stared at the peaceful face; she needed more. Gently, she held the hilt of the blade and then yanked it out. Blood squirted up and the amount doubled to leak out of the wound.

Don's eyes popped open and he groaned. "Jeezus Christ," he exclaimed. "Let me die in peace!"

"Not until you give me something useful. No bullshit." Christine held the blade above his crotch.

"An empty threat," he coughed and chuckled. "But, do me a favor. Please?"

Christine nodded.

Don smiled weakly. "Get the bastards who set us up."

"Who? Give me names."

"Adriana Prado...she isn't Cuban Intelli..." he stopped talking as he took a deep shuddering breath. "Intelligence, but for Esposito..." Christine was about to speak when he grabbed her hand. He looked frantic. "CI has been disbanded for years. Esposito doesn't need it when he has...he has..."

His voice faded away as life finally left him.

Christine knelt there staring at the dead body. She didn't know what to do.

"Dios mio! What have you done?"

Juan de Dios limped onto the roof, his face shocked and startled by the sight that greeted him. He made short time to get over to where the body and Christine was. He grabbed her arm and hauled her to her feet. "Have you gone mad? You know you have doomed us all now."

Christine didn't say a word. She stared at the old man.

"Come on," Juan said. "Once more, I must clean up after you."

He turned and began to limp his way back over to the stairwell. When he realized that Christine was not following him, he sighed and then looked back. "Christine, vamos!"

She shook her head. "Not just yet."

Juan shooked his head. "¡Por el amor del Dios!"

He stormed back over to her and roughly grabbed her arm. "You are a silly girl and... Dios mio!" He let go of her arm and quickly backed away.

Christine smiled as the once dead body of Don, screamed back to life and shuddered. The eyes blinked open and stared blankly at her. "There we go," she said to herself.

"What on Earth is happening?" Juan was practically babbling and calling for his mother.

"I told you," Christine said with calmness and joy at being proven right. Slowly, she stood up and watched as the Zombie-Don shambled to its feet. From the knife wound, intestines started to unravel. Like the others she had seen, the skin was pale and slightly more translucent.

"Kill it!"

She turned her head slightly to glare at Juan. That was her mistake.

Her eyes flicked back just in time to see Zombie-Don lunge at her. Both went down with him on top, snarling, biting, and clawing at her face. His teeth were slightly yellow now.

Christine kicked out, trying to flip him off her, but his weight was too much and he kept her pinned. His mouth was lightning fast as he tried to bite into her flesh. She screamed as she strained to dodge the attacks.

A mighty hit from Juan's cane sent Zombie-Don rolling off Christine. She coughed and watched as the old man hurried over and began to stab the undead body with the end of the cane. It easily slid into the deceased flesh. Again and again he stabbed while the zombie growled and shrieked. Violent and disgusting looking, Juan's attacks were completely useless.

"Juan, you're not doing anything," Christine said as she took the bloodied cane from the old man. "Like this," and with a single stab, Christine Moore rammed the end of the cane through the skull and into the brain. Zombie-Don shuddered and when she wrenched the cane out, the creature died.

Panting, she turned to Juan. "Let's go."

CHAPTER SEVENTEEN

It hadn't taken long for the authorities to cordon off the area surrounding the factory. President Sanderson had been escorted quickly and quietly back to the Saratoga while the body was removed and the entire building searched.

Juan had taken Christine out the back. He looked shell-shocked, as if he was questioning everything he had ever been told in his entire life. Christine knew he wanted to ask her what had happened, but his initial instincts were to be furious with her. It wasn't until one of his minions approached him with the carry case and Don's notebook which was covered in blood that he remembered who he was and what had happened earlier during the tour.

The old spy master tried to pry it open, but after being in the sun for too long, the blood had dried. Christine had covered her giggles by coughing at the sight. He stared daggers at her then casually put it and the case into the trunk of his Coup Deville. "He'll want to see this."

"Who?" Christine asked. "Who will want to see it? Esposito? Jeremiah Banks?"

Juan turned to her then reached over and grabbed her arm. "Get in and be quiet."

They drove in silence. Juan didn't even have the radio on. He gripped the wheel tightly, his knuckles white. His face was set in a grim stare. Christine had to keep brushing the hair out of her eyes, the wind was that strong. "Do you want to talk about what happened?"

"No. No, I don't." The old man's voice was definite. Something had snapped in him during the attack, something that made Christine uneasy. So she tried a different track.

"Where are we going, Juan?"

"¡Cállate!" He snapped as he steered the car onto the Malecón.

Across the sea wall out towards the Caribbean were thick dark clouds. Christine could see the waves being kicked up. There were periodic flashes of lightning and she had one thought, *If it rains, please let us be indoors.*

The car started to slow and Juan looked for a place to park. It didn't take long and the car came to a sharp shuddering stop. He looked at the beautiful spy next to him. "Get out."

Christine did as she was told then watched as the old man followed. He held out his arm to her and they slowly walked together. "I tried to tell you about them. That something was happening. You wouldn't believe me. It's not just here either, Juan. All over Cuba…zombies. I still can't fucking say it without laughing. Zombies are in Cuba."

She waited for the old man to answer her as the continued to walk along the Malecón. The sea wall was built in sections. Juan kept looking at each one. Christine soon realized that he was never going to talk about the monsters. She sighed. "What are you looking for?"

"This!" he answered with a wave of his walking stick. The tip of it pointed to a slightly misshapen slab. "Go, mira."

Christine wasn't sure about any of this. Tentatively, she stepped towards it, her head moving around, scanning for any threats.

"If I was going to kill you, do you think I would do it in public? Give me some credit."

The woman smiled apologetically and stared at the concrete section. It was like all the others, nondescript in nearly every way except for the two corners pointed to sea being eroded. Christine could not see anything of importance about it. "I don't see anything."

"¡Aye, por favor!" Juan hissed as he limped over to her. Using the stick, he tapped the face of it. A dull metallic click could be heard. "There."

Bending down, Christine saw a small rectangular plaque. It was old and withered. With a sinking feeling somewhere between abject terror and disbelief in her stomach, her eyes ran over the inscription:

FOR THE FALLEN UNJUST
THE STATION HOUSE IS ALWAYS
OPEN TO YOU.

"This is to be your fate, mi amor," Juan said softly, "if you continue to fight me. I am not your enemy."

Christine was sobbing as she rose to her feet. She took the perfectly folded linen kerchief from Juan and dried her eyes. "I thought their bodies were never found."

The old man nodded. "They never were."

"Then...?"

"Station Master forbade it. Something about no traces of his operatives ever. ¡Al carajo! No old foreigner pendejo is going to tell me what I can and cannot do on my own soil!" Juan was livid with the memory. "I am the head of Cuban Intelligence! I decide what I do! So I had this erected in tribute."

Christine hugged the old man. His arms went up to defend himself then stopped when he realized what was happening. He smiled as he gently disentangled himself from her. "No thanks required, but you are going to have a plaque here, if you're not careful."

She nodded. "But why bring me here now? You've had plenty of chances."

"Blame the foolishness of age," Juan said as he rubbed his face suddenly tired. "I thought that you were going to be able to handle yourself. Like you used to. Alas..."

Christine puffed herself up. "I've been doing fine, thank you. It would have been better if you and Adriana had not—"

"Adriana?" Juan asked, his eyes blazing. "What is that puta doing here? Why are you working with her? Are you a pinche idiota?"

"Cuidate, old man," Christine said softly. "She has been more helpful than you. At least she went to Guantanamo Bay."

Juan had to sit on one of the concrete sections he was laughing so much. "You blind fool." He continued to laugh until he was attacked by a coughing fit. "Guantanamo is no longer in operation," he said finally.

Christine stood there shocked. Slowly, she sank next to Juan.

"You're really in over your head," he said sweetly.

"But...but...she told me what happened."

Juan de Dios shook his head. "Let's start at the beginning. Remember?"

Christine chuckled. "I'm not fresh out of the gate "

"But you are," Juan said gently. "You are acting the same way." He cleared his throat. "This is the problem with growing old. You can see the mistakes of youth so much clearer than your own..." He turned and stared out at the coming storm. "Do you know why I was so vexed with you on the roof? Don't shake your head stupidly. Either answer or keep quiet." His tone wasn't harsh but that of a teacher. "That man you had killed was working for me."

"What?!"

Juan nodded and patted Christine's hand. "Niña, let me ask you this. Have you ever trusted Station Master? Think carefully before answering."

Christine looked up, the sky was growing darker and the clouds looked ominous. She thought about everything Station Master had said to her, the way he ran The Station. "I didn't think so," she heard Juan say.

"But he said that Station Master was going to hire him."

"A ruse setup by myself, unfortunately. In this day and age, Cuba is still regarded as being untrustworthy in the eyes of the espionage world. I had to use trickery. The idiot should never have told you!" Juan sniffed the air. "It's going to be a mighty impressive rapture... Why did Adriana come to you?"

"I'm sorry for your man," Christine apologized, "but why have him here anyway?"

Juan looked sheepish as he spoke. "To keep tabs on you. But why, Christine? Why on Earth did you have to maim him?"

"I had met him before. He was the one delivering the intel that brought The Station back to Cuba."

The old man nodded his head. "The Station never left," he said softly.

"What?"

"Nada," he said a little too quickly. "Tell me about Adriana."

Christine closed her eyes and tilted her head up as the wind came rushing in. It was cool and felt wonderful on her skin. The smells of Cuba mingled with that of rain and the sea was the perfect perfume that she would have gladly worn. "The old man said that CI would give me a contact to work with here. I should have gone straight to you. But she came to me, claiming to be back in your good graces. I didn't want to believe her, yet she kept appearing and she helped. The day of Pinar del Rio? She said she went to the Bay."

"And she told you some story about how she got in and found or didn't find anything of value?"

Christine nodded. "We had been informed that there was WMDs there." She glanced at Juan; his face was incredulous.

"And you believed it?"

"I had to follow up any leads that might get me closer to saving him."

"President Sanderson?"

Again, she nodded. "Since there was no—"

"Never has been."

"Says you." Christine hated to be interrupted. She knew that if Juan continued like this, then he would have everything he needed, but for what, she could not tell. But she wasn't going to let it happen. "When did CI get disbanded?" she said slowly and deliberately.

"What? Who said...?" Juan trailed off, his face falling. "That is of no importance."

Christine scoffed as a flash of lightning struck the waves. "From the moment I got here, you have been leading me around like a dog! Why, Juan? What could have possessed you to lie to me?"

Juan looked tiny now; he fiddled with his walking stick, trying not to look at her.

"Answer me!"

He sighed. "I am an old man who has made many many

mistakes over the years. This," he tapped the plaque, "being my worst. My noble presidente decided that Cuba didn't need a secret police. He was worried we were going to become like the Tonton Macoute. I was fired, my network disbanded, and that was it. Since then, I've been waiting to die."

"What? This your last attempt to be relevant?" Christine would have felt sympathy for the man, but there was a part of her that needed to see him broken.

"No." Juan was shaking his head rapidly. "The moment poor Rafael called me, telling me you were back, I knew I had the chance; my last chance to get forgiveness."

Then it all made sense to her. "That's why you brought me here."

"And to tell you the truth."

Christine wanted to know but spite rose to her mouth. "What? That Adriana works for Esposito? That this is all a setup and Jeremiah Banks is your best friend?"

"Por favor!" the old man wailed over the thunder. "I am an old man, Christine, have mercy."

"Like you had mercy on my friends?" She laughed harshly. "I should never have trusted you. Like everyone else deceitful!"

She stood and stared out at the tempest fast approaching them. For some reason, it calmed her, but only slightly. Juan started sobbing, and inherently Christine knew this was her moment to bring up the zombies. She sat down next to the old man and gently held his hand.

"It's been one hell of a day. Shit, the last couple of days have been up there."

"Up where," the old man asked, looking at the sky.

Christine laughed. "Not literally. Up there, like, in the top ten list of worst days ever."

Juan nodded. "I can count the number of them on my hand." He rubbed his face. "You should never have come back."

"What?"

"La muerte te sigue."

Christine laughed. "The fuck is that supposed to mean?"

Juan de Dios looked at her. "Exactly that. Make of it what you will. I'm too old and tired for this."

"Why would Death be following me?"

"Ask the man you call Station Master."

Christine shook her head as a loud thunderclap sounded, followed by lightning strikes. The storm had officially hit Havana. "I've got a job to do," she said more to herself than to the spy master. In a way, it was to remind herself the real reason she was here.

"A job?"

"Yeah, save the president and kill Jeremiah Banks." Saying it out loud again made her feel in control, something she hadn't felt since arriving.

"Look around!" Juan had to scream to be heard. "¡Cuba, se dirige a la condenación!"

Christine ignored the shouts as she fought against the howling winds, making her way down the Malecón.

#

Goddamn that old man, Christine thought as she sat at the bar in the Nacional. Her ashtray had the half-smoked remains of a Montecristo Doble Edmundo. Beside it was a mojito that she had barely touched. She looked around; since the storm had come in proper, the bar had slowly started to fill up. It was now almost at capacity and Christine's foul mood had not improved.

A couple of young Cubans and gringos tried to speak with her but after a few choice insults aimed at their manhoods, Christine was left alone.

"Damn La Perpetua," a businessman sitting beside her said to his partner. "Buying up every cigar factory and crumbling building. Do you know who owns it?"

"Not a clue," his friend said. "But did you hear it brought Guantanamo Bay from the USA?"

Christine turned slightly at that. Her mind raced; if this was true, then chances were she could get to the base. "Excuse me," she said in her most apologetic voice, "you just said that La Perpetua has been buying buildings and companies and now the base and I don't mean to pry but…what is La Perpetua?"

The two businessmen looked at the woman then to each other. The first gave a big smile before answering, "It's new. Privately owned and has been slowly buying land here since Obama started to talk with Castro. Why would a dish like you want to know?" He leaned forward and his eyes lingered on Christine's bosom.

"Just curious. Lots of people are talking about them. I didn't think that a US company could buy property and businesses in Cuba?"

The second younger shook his head. "It's not US. It used to be then apparently a while ago it relocated and was restructured. Now its base of operations is Mexico. Smart move really."

"Indeed. Especially if you take into account the Guantanamo purchase," Big Smile said as he tried to stroke Christine's hand.

"Oh?" she asked, casually using that hand to take a sip from her drink.

"Well, it makes sense," Big Smile replied, trying to impress the woman. "The USA has been using the base for renditions and as a detention center for years. Ever since way back in the 1940s during Batista. Nowadays, with the way the global relations scene has been going, they can't afford to anymore. Look at it from the UN's point of view, if a superpower—"

"They haven't been that for ages," Young One muttered.

"A superpower," Big Smile continued, "has bases in another country to run espionage operations, renditions, and have it as its own torture room, that is bad for business. On a global level. Yes yes yes, all countries do it. But if the country is trying to get a better reputation, then removing such a base from another land would be great for PR. Then if you take into account the fact that La Perpetua has been making releases about all the new equipment, housings, and jobs it will create... It's obvious that whoever has a vested interest in Cuba and American talks, this is the perfect move."

Christine nodded, but her mind was elsewhere. Now she knew two things; the first was that she had been wrong all this time. Money. That was the name of the game. Secondly, she had to now get to Guantanamo Bay.

"Disculpe, señora?" the bartender said, tapping her arm. "Señora? Telefono." He laid the phone on the bar in front of her then went back to chatting up some floozies.

Christine picked up the phone then with a smile she turned away from the two businessmen. "Bueno."

"Chris! Thank God, are you okay? Did he hurt you again?"

"Adriana," Christine said, "how quickly can you get here?"

"Five minutes."

"See you out front...and bring a car!"

"Si," Adriana said, "Pero, ¿a dónde vamos?"

Christine allowed herself a small smile. "Field trip."

#

"Some field trip," Adriana muttered as the Chevrolet careened along the highway. "Can you please get us away from the coast!"

Christine was driving, hands glued to the wheel and eyes on the road. The storm buffeted the old car. "When I can."

The moment Adriana had pulled up in front of the Nacional, Christine dove in, pushed Adriana into the passenger seat then took off. Very little had been said between them.

"You were right about Juan."

"Gracias!" Adriana bowed her head slightly. "Mira, I'm not just a pretty face."

She reached out and gently squeezed Christine's thigh. The blonde grinned stupidly as she turned the wheel. The car was now driving along a small one-lane road. It had been asphalted, recently too. *Good*, Christine thought.

"Chris, where are we going?" Adriana asked softly.

"It's a surprise," Christine said. "A really good one."

Adriana said nothing as she looked around, her face screwed up slightly as she tried to figure out where they were headed. After a moment, she shook her head, "No sé."

Christine didn't make any comment; instead, she pressed further down on the accelerator, propelling the old classic car faster and faster. Whoever had owned it before Adriana had done a bang-up job of keeping it in almost pristine condition. There was a slight rattle that had started to annoy her. Other than that, she quite enjoyed the experience of driving it.

"So," Adriana said, trying to sound causal, "how did you get the stalwart Juan de Dios to talk?"

A humorless chuckle came from Christine. "Emotional blackmail."

The Cuban nodded. "Care to elaborate?"

Christine shook her head. She had a plan and nothing was

going to get in the way. It had become night and Christine had no idea what time it was. The pelting rain didn't help the situation either.

Even though the car was in good condition, the tires needed to be changed. Almost bald, they had trouble gripping the slick wet road. Christine felt these as she drove and had to make minor adjustments to compensate.

"Chris," Adriana said after a quick glance out the back, "I don't want to alarm you, but we've got a stalker."

Lights flashed behind them, reflecting in the rearview mirror. Christine had to squint. The driver of the car meant business.

"Hold tight."

Christine slammed booth feet down on the break.

The wheels jammed and the Chevrolet spun.

Its front bumper caught the other car's, a small Dodge, passenger side. As both vehicles continued their rollercoaster trip, Christine peered at the other driver. In the darkness, she couldn't see much, just a panama hat and maybe a flash of gray.

"Fuck me!" Adriana screamed as Christine fought with the vehicle to get it back under control. The old tires screeched and kicked out each time she turned the wheel.

Christine kept one eye on the road and the other on the Dodge. It had stopped spinning and came to a stop. Waiting.

"Straighten up!"

"I will if you shut your mouth!"

Christine had one foot on the brake and the other on the gas pedal. She tapped each one consecutively until the car stopped spinning.

They were pointing backwards. Christine shifted the gears into reverse then put pedal to the metal.

The driver of the Dodge didn't know what to make of the view he got: A Chevrolet speeding in reverse past him, the driver giving him the finger and the passenger blowing kisses.

Christine kept speeding until the other car's lights had disappeared.

"You think we are safe?" Adriana asked.

"Yep, he won't be following us anytime soon."

"How do you know?"

Christine started laughing as she put the car in the right direction then they were off. "His back wheels are in a ditch."

Adriana allowed herself a chuckle. "Who do you think it was?"

Christine shrugged as they turned onto a more used road. "You tell me."

"What does that mean?" Adriana sounded indignant.

Christine didn't answer. Her eyes were on the road. "Here we are."

#

The rain had stopped, but the clouds were still dark and deep with the occasional rumble of thunder to remind them to hurry. Christine and Adriana got out of the car. Christine walked towards a gate and fumbled with something.

"Where the hell are we?" Adriana asked again, getting exasperated with the lack of response.

Christine turned around then walked over to the Cuban. She thrust what appeared to be a small metal sign at Adriana. "You should know. Liar."

Adriana looked down at the sign:

GUANTANAMO BAY
PRIVATE PROPERTY
SOLD

"This must be the other side," Adriana said a little too quickly. "I always enter from the south."

"This is the fucking south," Christine said as she started to climb the fence. "Come on," she ordered.

They didn't take long to make it across the sandy patch that used to be a minefield. Christine had picked up a handful of pebbles and used them to check for any of the bombs. She flicked them left and right and as each one landed, both women held their breath. Not a single explosion.

After getting in through the main door which had been left open, no need to worry about security now, Christine went to find a map. "You've been here before; the other day, in fact. Right?"

Adriana stood there looking like a child caught with their hand in the candy jar. "Si, por que?"

Christine grabbed two flashlights from a utility closet and handed one to Adriana. "You lead then."

The Cuban took a breath then started walking.

Each room they came had been completely cleaned out. Not even a scrap of paper had been left. Adriana would scan a room quickly then move onto the next. Christine, on the other hand, made sure to inspect the rooms thoroughly. There was a layer of dust on all the exposed surfaces.

"Did it look like they were cleaning out the place the other day?"

Adriana shook her head. "No. It was business as always. I wonder what happened?"

A snort from Christine. "Obviously, they got word we were coming and so they had to vacate the premises."

"En serio?"

Christine stopped. "Don't play dumb with me. La Perpetua brought the base. That's why there was a 'sold' sticker on that sign... Or did you fail to notice it?"

Before Adriana could answer, Christine stormed past her. "Why, Adriana? Why all the lies?"

"What do you mean, cariña?"

Christine found a small filing cabinet and started going through it. "You should have told me about CI, about your government job, fucking everything!"

Adriana said nothing. She watched as Christine finished going through the files. Nothing. In frustration, Christine slammed the drawers shut then gave it a kick. "Well?"

A long sigh escaped from Adriana "I was under orders. When Esposito got word about a Station agent coming back to Cuba, we had to make sure that whoever it was would be on the level. He ordered me not to break cover at all. I didn't know it was going to be you, Chris..."

"What a story! I believe every word of it." Christine's voice dripped with sarcasm and contempt. "Or maybe this is another cover and really you're a double for the USA." She stormed down a corridor then down some stairs. Adriana had to run to catch up with her.

"You know how much I hate the gringos! Remember all the long talks we had?"

Christine's face was like stone. "How do I know anything is true?"

"You don't," Adriana said, tears streaming down her face. "All you can do is go on a little faith."

Christine stopped. They had come to a dead end. A foreboding cement wall glared at them. Adriana was breathing hard and fast. Christine sensed they were close to something.

"A little faith? Fine," Christine said, turning to look at her former lover. She took Adriana's face in her hands and held it tightly. "Answer me this one question truthfully and I'll give you all my faith."

Adriana nodded the best she could, her eyes darting between Christine and the wall.

"Why didn't you come here?"

Christine watched as the Cuban tried to look truthful. It did not suit her, and to Christine, it was obviously fake. "Never mind." She turned and started down another passageway.

"Espera."

Christine stopped but did not turn. "What is it?"

Adriana was beside her. "Come with me."

#

Christine followed Adriana. They hadn't spoken much and the emptiness of the base was getting to Christine. "You going to tell me where we're going?"

"Here," Adriana said as she opened a door.

The room was covered in blood. Pools of it littered the floor. The walls were smeared with blood and tissue. Christine stared at the sight. "What happened here?"

"A training exercise, as far as CI knows. Someone got injured, then died. This," she gestured at the room, "is what happened after."

"How do you know?" Christine asked as she stepped over the pools. Her eyes were on scorch marks.

"My contact sent me an email. Apparently, they had to evacuate the base. That's why I didn't go... Zombies are fucking real, Chris!"

Christine's eyes scanned the scorch marks. Her mind putting it all together. "They had to burn everyone!"

Adriana stayed at the doorway. Her expression was one of horror and disgust. "My contact told me that from the one hundred and fifty people stationed here, only twenty-five made it out alive. The sale is just a cover-up."

Christine turned back to the Cuban agent. "Only if you believe that. La Perpetua might be the ones responsible for this."

"Why? What would they have to do with destroying Cuba?"

Christine laughed. "Once a capitalist. Always a capitalist."

Adriana laughed with her. "That's the motto of the gringos. Right?"

"If it isn't, then it should be." Both chuckled as they stepped out of the room. Christine turned to her. "Wait. If you knew about this, then why not alert your superiors? Or the Americans?"

Adriana sighed. "What makes you think I didn't? You may call me a bitch looking out for herself, but I do care and love my country." Something had cracked inside the Cuban and what she was saying, at least to Christine, was at last the truth.

"That may all be true, but if you had, then there would be no festival. No presidential visit. And, most importantly, no me being here."

A loud clang broke the tension. Both women spun towards the sound. It echoed throughout the empty rooms and corridors. "You think we're alone?"

"Jodido si lo sé," Adriana answered as she slowly moved into the corridor. "Pero no estoy esperando para averiguarlo."

Christine had to agree. What originally had started out as an almost normal mission had slowly become a total clusterfuck. The last thing she needed was for this to turn into a bad zombie movie. Another loud bang echoed and Christine thought, *Shit maybe it already had.* "Let's get outta here."

Together, they started back towards the entrance. At each corner and doorway, they would peer around, checking for the slightest hint of another soul, or something worse.

The banging was getting louder and sounding faster and faster. At each noise, Christine and Adriana quickened their pace.

They could hear the thunderstorm above them and both were

thankful nothing had attacked them.

"We're so close," Adriana exulted as they neared the main door.

"Maybe. Maybe not. But there is still this fucked-up situation to sort out."

The Cuban nodded her agreement. "But how do we stop…whatever is happening?"

As Christine opened the door, she turned to look at Adriana. "Not my job. I'm here for…" She frowned at the expression Adriana had. "Adriana?"

Her counterpart had her eyes wide, and she started to shake her head wildly.

Christine had no idea what was going on.

Adriana lifted a hand then pointed.

Christine turned towards the cement wall and her mouth dropped open.

"Hola, chicas," Juan de Dios said casually. Then he fired the Taser.

CHAPTER EIGHTEEN

Waves.

The melodic sounds of the water lapping, gently rising and falling, slapping against hard surfaces is what woke Christine. Her eyes fluttered open then quickly clamped closed. The sun's light was blinding and she had to blink a few times before it was comfortable to keep them open.

Her chest ached like a son-of-a-bitch. It felt like a power point had raped her.

Christine reached up. Her arm stopped. She strained then gave up. It was strapped to her side. Checking the other arm gave the same result. "Fuck."

Slowly, Christine rocked back then forward. Her body screamed for her to stop. But she couldn't. Her legs pressed down on the slatted wooden floor and she found herself in an upright seated position.

The boat was lovely. Expensively exquisite; not exactly a super yacht but close enough. The wood surfaces were the best money could buy. Every surface had been polished until it was clear and showed an almost perfect reflection. This was the vessel of a person with more money than sense.

"About time you woke up," Adriana said. She too was bound but not with straps. Her hands were tied with cable ties. There was a bruise on her face that covered her left eye. Her lip had a cut and there was a slight trail of blood running down her ear.

"What the fuck happened?" Christine asked, her eyes scanning for signs of anyone.

Adriana tilted her head upwards in a short gesture. Christine followed the gaze then wished she hadn't.

The sun was right behind the figure. There was something familiar about him. In one hand, there was the distinct shape of an old Colt handgun and the other was resting atop the walking stick.

"Juan," Christine cursed.

The old man nodded then started to walk down the stairs leading from the canopy controls to the deck. He moved slowly. Each step he took had to be steady so that he wouldn't fall down the stairs or trip over his walking stick.

Both Christine and Adriana glared at the traitor. Juan smiled pleasantly as he leaned against the railing. He kept the pistol aimed at the women. "Buenas dias."

Adriana spat venom. "¡Tienes dos cara mentirosas mierda! ¿Te llamas hombre? ¡Un perro rabioso es más digno de confianza que usted! ¡Has traicionado todo lo que creías! ¡Traidor!"

"Por favor," Juan said lazily as he walked over to the Cuban and with no thought pistol-whipped her.

Adriana toppled over from the force. Her cheek cut opened, blood splattered the wood paneling. She grunted then tried to get herself right side up. Christine got to her knees. "Coward!"

Juan turned to her with a chuckle. "Coward? Is it cowardly to realize that your country will never give you the respect you deserve or the treatment? Is it cowardly to want a better life? Is it cowardly to become a capitalist?"

"Not at all," Christine replied casually, "but it is to beat a woman."

Juan's smile faded. "I am sorry for that. My Mama raised me better than this. She would say 'Juanito...' that's what she would call me... 'Juanito, in this life you can be happy or smart.' For many many years, I was happy. Now I am smart." He looked down at Christine's chest. "Does it hurt?"

Adriana struggled to get back upright. "Yeah, come over here and let me show you how much, puto!"

Juan turned to her then raised his weapon. "I didn't have to bring you with us," he said. "My orders were to bring the pariah." He placed the gun and the walking stick on the deck then pulled Adriana to a sitting position. "Now behave."

She smashed her head into his, her forehead connecting with his nose. There was a sickening crack followed by a crunch. Blood spurted up and out. In a beautiful arch, it landed on the railing and into the crystal clear blue water.

Juan fell backwards with a cry of pain, one hand holding his broken nose, the other frantically grasping for the pistol. "Pendeja!"

The pistol flashed up and came to a stop inches away from Adriana's face. She smiled and Christine giggled.

Juan's face was flushed with anger and he growled. "Listen to me, jintera! One more stunt like that and the fishes will feast." He cocked the weapon. "¿Entiendo?"

Adriana yawned. "You won't kill me, niñito."

Juan laughed and looked between the two women. "Pray tell why?"

Christine caught the look in Adriana's eye. "Because," she quickly said, "then you wouldn't be able to lord it over us."

"Si!" Adriana joined in. "Kill me and your audience becomes one. That's boring, right? You love having an audience. A performer like you!" She turned to Christine. "Did you know what he did before joining CI?"

Christine shook her head. Adriana pulled a shocked face. "You don't? He never told... Juan! Why didn't you ever tell Chris?"

Juan de Dios looked embarrassed. "It never came up in conversation."

"I have all the time in the world now," Christine said, trying to look nonchalant.

"Our Juanito here," Adriana said, using the name Juan's mother called him, "used to be one of Cuba's greatest actors!"

"En serio!"

Juan nodded. "Acting, singing, and a little bit of dancing. I was going to be the greatest. The stage was my family and soon there was going to be movies! But...then, CI came and recruited me, wanted me to infiltrate Castro's little band of killers. Then, after the Revolution, they kept me on."

"Why not continue? Surely the people remember you?" Christine asked, partly out of interest and partly to continue distracting him.

The old man sighed. "The only people who remember the good old days of Juan de Dios are long gone. The only people who remember me are puto cinefiles and hipsters."

Adriana and Christine sighed. "Poor, poor thing," Christine cried. "You must miss it. Performing."

"Si, but in a way, this is the greatest performance of my life. You, Christine, were the audience and you ate up my performance completely. There is no other feeling greater than this. It is better than sex!" Juan was practically taking a bow.

"And that is why you can't kill me." Adriana brought the distraction full circle. "Imagine, before you reveal the master plan, a monologue of such exquisite words, you kill me. Then your oration would be before one, which is fine if you prefer that. But two? Imagine both of our reactions."

Juan laughed. "Your training in the whorehouse really was superb." He looked her up and down. "I'm glad I tried you out before recruiting you... What?" The old man looked from Adriana to Christine and a cruel smile spread across his face. "You didn't know?"

He started to laugh, and if Christine had the ability to break her bonds, then she would have done so gladly, then after breaking Juan's arms, she would remove his genitals and making sure he was bleeding sufficiently enough, Christine would throw him overboard. Instead, she said, "It doesn't matter. You're just trying to get under both our skins." She shook her head. "Pathetic."

Juan thought while staring at the two ladies. His eyes kept lingering on Adriana who had gone silent. Since the revelation, her head hung low, tears streaming down her beaten face; there were small sobs coming from her and she was slumped, completely broken. The ex-spy master looked at Christine. "You had her. I know you have. Could you taste men?"

"That's enough, Juan," a velvety voice said from behind the old man. Juan straightened, his hand clenched the grip of the handgun, and he started sweating instantly. Slowly, he turned to face the owner of the voice.

#

Jeremiah Banks looked like a disappointed father. He wore

linen pants with flip-flops and a light blue, long-sleeve shirt. His hair was graying at the temples and even though he wore a friendly smile on the perfectly manicured bearded face, which was also tinged with gray, his eyes were cold and hard; ice blue like steel. "Why don't you get a drink?" he suggested to Juan. His voice was velvet and deep with a gruffness that betrayed his low-upbringing.

Juan de Dios nodded and as he walked past Banks, he muttered something. Christine couldn't hear what he said, but the way Jeremiah Banks looked at her made her think that she was going to die here. Banks watched as Juan disappeared into the cabin.

"Please forgive me for the poor reception," he said as he undid Adriana's bonds. Slowly, he helped her up and to a seat. The Cuban was still silent but now the sobbing had stopped. Banks tilted her head up and proceeded to inspect her wounds. His face clouded over. "I told him not to hurt you."

Christine watched the man who had caused all her misery and her mind screamed for her to tear out his jugular. She growled and strained against her restraints. Banks continued to tenderly check on Adriana and that made her angrier; not what he had done, but that now he was taking care of her. The man must be made to suffer.

"Don't worry, Miss Moore. I'll get to you soon." He sighed as Adriana brushed his hands away then he turned to the captive. "At last we meet!" Banks sounded genuinely happy to meet her, like a fan. "I would shake your hand, but I don't think that would be beneficial to me." He chuckled then sat next to Adriana.

"What do you want with me?"

"Straight to the point. Good. Everyone said that's how you are." Banks gestured around them. "Look around you, Miss Moore. Tell me, what do you see?"

Christine strained to see around her. She hadn't before and silently cursed herself for a rookie mistake. The boat was in Havana Bay and Christine could see La Cabaña on the left and the towers of the Nacional. In the distance, music could be heard, a band practicing. There were other boats in the bay but no one was on deck.

"Miss Moore?" Banks' voice got her attention.

"Cuba," she said. "I see the heart of Cuba. Her soul... And I see the cancer that has been slowly killing her."

Banks was nodding. "The Americans. Yes! You don't disappoint! The Americans ARE a cancer that has spread across the globe. Luckily, they haven't infected Cuba like the rest of the Caribbean." Banks scratched his bearded chin. "Were it possible to wipe them from the planet, I would. But, Cuba is just as good."

Christine didn't know what to make of Banks. Was he crazy or just acting like it? "I was talking about you."

Banks stopped, blinked, then started to laugh. "They said you had a sense of humor... But seriously, Miss Moore, can I call you Christine?"

"No."

"Well, Christine, you have not disappointed me. Just so you know that. From the files and reports about you, your reputation has been well earned. My partner was right about you."

Partner? That was curious. Why would a criminal syndicate leader have a partner? Security maybe, someone in a position of legal power perhaps. She smiled as she said, "La Perpetua, how long have you been setting this up?"

"Would you believe me if I said, not that long at all." Banks glanced at Juan who had returned. "Your gun please."

"What if they try something?" Juan's face was a little panicky and he held onto the gun like it was a security blanket.

"I think we can assume they aren't going to... Juan, your gun."

Slowly, the old man let the gun slip from his fingers and into the open palm of his boss. "Thank you," Banks said. "Now why don't you get on the radio and find out where Sanderson is? That's a good fellow."

Again, Juan went back into the cabin. Banks hefted the weapon thoughtfully. "What do you know about La Perpetua?"

"In English, it means 'Perpetual.' It's a good name," Christine admitted, "but why all this? Our intel said that you had gone, disappeared. Why come back?"

Banks got off the chair and bent before Christine. "I never left."

"You are a pendejo," Adriana said softly. Banks and Christine turned to see her. Adriana was sitting slightly more upright and her face was like stone.

"Excuse me?" Banks looked confused and Christine hoped her partner had a play.

"Tu eres un pendejo," she said again. "What gives you the right to play Lord of Cuba?"

"The right?" he repeated. "What gives any man the right to lord over a country? A people? Democracy? No. Tradition? No. Birth? No. What gives a man the right to do anything is Strength of Will."

"Puto," Adriana spat. "That's what a bully thinks."

"And the biggest bully is across that water," Banks said, pointing to the city. There was something about this that felt familiar to Christine. A distant memory was trying to get her attention.

"He's seeing El Presidente today and tomorrow," Juan reported sullenly. "Tomorrow night, he will be at PabExpo for the closing dinner. She can do it there."

"Very good, Juan. Please go and wait in your cabin. When I'm finished with our guests, you will get your payment."

"Do what?"

The men ignored Christine's question. There was tension in the air between them and it felt like they were having a silent battle.

"No," Juan said. "I want it now."

"Come again?"

Juan stood next to Adriana and there was a flash of silver and a small stiletto blade was at her neck. "You have made me into something abhorrent," the old man said. "I have betrayed my country. My familia, my historia, and myself. For what? For more money than a man can spend in five lifetimes. I want it all. Now. Or the girl dies." He pressed the tip of the blade into the supple skin and droplets of blood started to seep down the fine neck.

"Forgive me," Banks said, "I thought I was dealing with a caballero, not some Haitian thug... Very well. You may have it all. What you have earned." He nodded.

Adriana's hands were faster than a snake. They wrapped around the old man. His eyes went wide and for the briefest of moments, it seemed like he was going to scream.

He gurgled and foamy blood erupted from his mouth. The stiletto blade was buried deep into his chest. There were four other tiny pinpricks that were deep and seeping blood.

Adriana kept hold of the dying man and then she moved to the side and pushed.

Juan de Dios sank to the bottom of Havana Bay, leaving nothing but a trail of inky blood and a second-rate bar.

Christine's eyes were wide as Banks went over to Adriana, handed her a handkerchief then after she had cleaned herself, he kissed her on the lips. "Go clean up."

Adriana smiled at him and as she went inside, her eyes caught the look of betrayal on Christine's face. Adriana Prado blew a kiss.

"Greed is good," Banks said, looking at the slowly dying ripples in the water. "But know when to bring it out for a walk."

"I'm going to kill you," Christine snarled.

"Don't be an idiot... You won't kill me the same way I won't kill you. We are both too valuable." He checked his watch. "You don't have much time, Christine. And failure is not an option when working for me."

"What is it you want me to do?"

Banks glanced at her. "Don't bog your mind down with needless details. All you need to know is that you have the most important job in the modern age. Succeed, and you will go down in history as a hero. Fail? Just another lunatic."

"What do you get out of this?" Christine asked, her mind trying to find something to latch onto; there was something about the way he spoke that made her want to be around him.

"Cuba. Do you know that the history of Cuba is almost as bloody as the history of Mexico? It is. The Spanish Conquistadors came to this island and did what they did to every new people they came across: destroyed them in the name of two things, Spain and Christianity. The books will say it was for gold and to become more dominant. But, in reality, they came because their God told them to. So, why, you ask, did they subjugate the natives? Easy. Spain needed servants. The Church needed new souls to preach at and condemn."

He paused as Adriana returned with drinks. Mojitos. She had

had a shower and was now wearing a bathrobe. "Let me untie her, so she can enjoy this."

Banks nodded and Adriana removed the restraints. Christine's wrists were bloodied and Adriana kissed one. Christine elbowed the Cuban in the face.

Adriana grunted then kicked Christine.

"That's enough," Banks said, pointing the gun at them. He gestured with it and Adriana moved back to his side.

Christine picked up the cocktail that had been placed beside her and took a small sip.

Banks smiled. "It's good, yes? Adriana makes the best mojitos in all of Cuba." He looked at the woman next to him and smiled. "Where was I?... Yes! Preaching and condemning. After Santiago, Trinidad, and Havana were built, the Spaniards needed workers. Slavery. It was a booming business in Cuba. They got them from the natives and from Africa, sold them to Haiti and the Dominican Republic. Then there was the Slave Revolution which pretty much showed Spain that Cuba would not be controlled by anyone."

"What has this got to do with me?"

"Patience child, patience." Banks spoke as a mentor does to a particularly slow student. "The battle with Spain brought in the Americans. This was the first proper time they had taken an active interest in Cuba."

"And then they came in and turned it into a degenerate hedonistic wonderland. Then Meyer Lansky placed Batista in power and the country became a cesspool like the USA. Right?" Adriana cut in; she looked bored beyond belief. Jeremiah Banks glared at her then turned back to Christine.

"This, is all about that. The way Cuba was is what it will become again IF the embargo is destroyed and Big Business with US money comes back to Cuba."

"What about La Perpetua?" Christine saw where this was going. "That's your money, right? Did you get it from here? Mexico or from your partners in the States?"

Banks chuckled. "Thank you, Christine." He turned to Adriana. "Be a dear and let Albert know the deal is almost done and that he should get to Havana now. Albert Bates," he said in response to Adriana's blank stare. She nodded then with a sad look to Christine she disappeared into the cabin.

"So, you see, Christine," Banks continued, "I'm not some terrorist or Bondian villain. All I am is a man who wants to protect his country. You could say I'm a Revolutionary."

"You want to protect Cuba," Christine repeated. "Protect Cuba?"

Banks nodded, proud that this woman was coming round to his way of thinking. "That's exactly what I'm trying to do."

Christine nodded, her face unreadable except for a slight glimmer of amusement. Luckily, Banks didn't notice it. "So, if you truly want to protect Cuba, which is quite a noble cause…" A part of her was worried that she was piling it on thick but in Christine's experience flattery was sometimes the best form of attack, "…then you must know about the plague?"

"Of course I do. People dying and then coming back to life, feeding on the flesh of the living, nothing more than the tales of the old and deranged. But, if you believe them, then there is a zombie plague," he said, laughing. "A mass hallucination from contaminated water and food. Or bad medicine." He winked at Adriana who shook her head.

"She's serious," the Cuban said. "I've seen it with my own eyes. That concierge. Rafael? Well, I saw him stand up and try to bite Chris' face. Nothing slowed him down."

"Not even having both arms hacked off," Christine added.

Both women looked at Banks, hoping for a reaction other than to think them crazy and kill them. They would have to do something. Anything. Soon. Adriana went first.

"No te estamos volviendo locos. Ahora mismo esto es más importante que tus planes." She shared a quick glance with Christine who gave a slight nod.

Jeremiah Banks looked out across the clear water at Havana. Absentmindedly, he stroked his beard.

"Y," Adriana pressed, "si no lo detenemos, muy pronto no habrá Cuba."

It started as a low chuckle, almost a snigger. Then it grew louder, more boisterous until Banks was bellowing with laughter. "Do you really expect me to believe this?" He turned to Adriana. "It's obvious that you've been turned!" He moved towards her.

"Bullshit," Christine's voice stopped him. "What if I can show you proof?"

"Proof of what? That you convinced her to betray me?"

Adriana snickered. "Really, Jerry? You've read my reports."

Banks looked at both women, studying each of them, his eyes darting back and forth. "Okay. Show me this proof."

Christine went over to where Juan had moments earlier stood. "Any moment, the late Juan de Dios is going to bob up all zombified." It felt odd to say that word. But in crazy times, you have to roll with it.

Instead of her desired reaction, Banks laughed, big guffaws. "They said you had a decent sense of humor. Zombies!" He clapped his hands. "Good. Good." He wiped away a fake tear then the smile vanished from his face replaced by a look that made Christine a little frightened. "You're going to need it soon, my dear."

A breeze had started up and it brought to the boat the smells of Havana. Christine took a deep breath and savored all the tastes. Her mind was racing. *He'll never believe us*, she thought. There was only one thing to do: Get off the boat without being killed. "Why? Are we going to a comedy club?"

Banks chuckled mirthlessly then with a quick one-two punch, Christine was doubled over. She clutched her belly and wheezed. "You listen to me. This isn't a game to be taken lightly. You saw what I did to Señor de Dios and your dear friends five years ago. Just imagine what we can do to you. ¿Entiendo?"

Christine nodded vigorously then winced as Banks dragged her to her feet. He looked at the city and sighed. "Forgive me. Sometimes my temper gets away."

The woman waved him away as if nothing had happened.

"You don't seem to understand," he said, "so let me put it in terms that will make you." He began to pace up and down the deck, brow furrowed and one hand in his pocket, the other stroking his beard. "If I was to come to you and say, 'For every person you killed, I would pay you five hundred thousand dollars,' how quick would it take you to figure out how many bullets you could spare?"

"What?"

"You. Kill. People. Five hundred thousand dollars per person." Banks spoke like the old Tarzan movies. "How many would you kill?"

"Jerry," Adriana had stuck her head out of the cabin and was looking at the man, "Señor Bates wants to talk to you."

Banks nodded then silently moved past Adriana and into the darkened room. The Cuban closed the sliding doors so as not to disturb him.

The two women stared at each other. The boat bobbed gently up and down, the rhythmic lapping of the waves and the breeze a relaxing force. Christine's fists were clenched tightly.

"It's ironic. Hm?" Adriana raised an eyebrow. "You come back to Havana with the goal to redeem yourself and now, this is the second time that I've… It's funny."

"Yeah, because I'm having a fucking riot," Christine growled. Her face was unreadable. She had to fight to keep herself from leaping across the deck and tearing the Cuban to pieces.

"Don't be like that, Chris. You know it's all about money."

Christine shook her head. "I bet the gringos would pay more for you to make sure nothing happens. Get a nice big shiny apartment along the Malecón? Suit you perfectly."

Adriana looked as if someone had just pissed on her leg and then told her that it was raining. "Jeremiah Banks is more Cuban than he is… Well, I don't know where he is from. But that's not important. What is is that it is better to be in bed with the devil, you know."

"And how many times has that happened?" Christine was hurt and getting close to lashing out.

"Never. He understands that this is just business."

Christine nodded her head while rolling her eyes. A boat full of young idiots floated lazily next to them. Christine ignored them as they called out, trying to get her attention. Adriana, on the other hand, went out of her way to make them feel welcome. She was just about to start offering them drinks when, "Honey, why do you play with these insects?"

Adriana laughed with a flick of her hair. "All boys must become men."

"But look at their trunks!" Christine pointed. "Not one of them looks like they can handle themselves." The boat's engines revved up and soon the insects were vanishing beyond the horizon.

The two ladies watched as the waves dispersed and became gentle again in the wake of the boat. Adriana started laughing while Christine went back to glowering at the Cuban.

"He does like the sound of his own voice," Adriana said with a small laugh changing the subject, "Jeremiah, I mean... Is he giving you the 'how many bullets' speech? He needs to stop being so verbose."

"Did he use it with you?"

Adriana nodded. "On me, Juan, pretty much everyone he needs to work for him."

"What was your answer to the question?"

"As many as it takes." Adriana smiled. "I'm going to skip ahead. Christine, you are going to kill President Sanderson."

Christine laughed, slapping her leg. She stood up then went over to where Adriana was resting against the rail. "I'll have another drink while I think. Okay?"

Adriana smiled and gently caressed Christine's arm. "Be right back."

Christine watched the sway of the Cuban's hips and for a moment allowed herself to smile.

After Adriana had left her sight, Christine started searching for a weapon. The storage compartments held nothing but the usual boating equipment, ropes, oars, life lines, vests, and more. She grumbled as there were no flare guns or anything she could actually use.

"Are you done yet?"

She spun around startled by Banks' voice. He leaned against the cabin wall with a slightly amused look. "Where's Adriana?"

"Making drinks," he said. "She mentioned that she told you what the job was. Well?"

"Give me details."

Banks shook his head. "Details. Details. Don't bog your mind down with unnecessary information. Trust that all will be well."

"Not on your life," Christine said as she moved to the stern railing. Resting her hands on it, she was ready for her next move.

"Why not? You'll be doing your beloved Cuba the greatest of

service plus you will never have to work again in your life. Retire to Santiago or Trinidad. Live on the beach until your dying days. Paradise is at your fingertips. All you have to do is say yes." There was a fervor to his words that was extremely compelling. Jeremiah Banks was a true believer.

Adriana returned and handed Banks and Christine their freshly made mojitos. She then stood next to her employer. "Has she agreed to it yet?"

Banks sipped his drink then shook his head. "She wants details, for some reason."

"Just tell her."

Christine watched the other boats. A part of her hoped for the Coastguard to make an appearance. But deep down, she knew that it would be futile.

"At the closing dinner, both presidents will be there. They are going to make an announcement that is going to change the way the world looks at Cuba. That cannot happen," Banks said conversationally.

"The last attempts haven't succeeded. Why change the game now?"

Banks nodded his approval. "Very good. Ever wondered why Cuba has never really tried to have the embargo removed? It's not because of Communism, nor is it because the people don't want it. By all means, most do want a better life that they think will come from US money. How wrong they are. No, the reason is much simpler. Tradition. Have you noticed that nearly all Latin American countries are steeped in tradition. Same here. For Cubans, not dealing with the US is tradition. And as we all know, traditions are hard to change. That is why I'm doing this. Because of traditions."

"And because no one else will," Christine asked. She was getting bored with all the monologuing.

Banks nodded and clapped his hands. "So, before the plan was to scare the president. But now, we have to be more direct. So at the dinner, you will kill him."

Christine raised herself up and sat on the railing. "How? Poison the food?"

"A sniper rifle and the position have all been set up for you at

PabExpo where the dinner is going to be held." Adriana started to move forward as both talked. Banks didn't notice. "This is the important part: he must be killed before either of them start talking. You'll know when the time will come."

"Jerry, maybe you should stop telling her everything?" Adriana said as she kept moving forward towards Christine.

"Don't be ridiculous," Christine said as she swung her feet. "Who am I going to tell?"

"I'd bet Station Master."

Banks let out a laugh. "I wouldn't worry about the Station anymore. Christine, what say you?"

She smiled at both. "I need time to think about it."

Jeremiah banks shook his head. "I need the answer now."

Adriana started to move faster, her mind realizing what was about to happen.

Christine grinned. "Then..."

She flipped backwards straight into the crystal clear water just as Adriana lunged for her.

CHAPTER NINETEEN

He hated the beach; always had ever since he was a child. Captain Mondragon would have been happy to never see sand again. But his esposa and niños could not keep away, so whenever they wanted to go, he always had work.

Not today though. The final day of the festival and for the life of him, the order had come down that the CIA was going to be patrolling the city, which meant one thing: the beach.

Juanito and Fabiola were frolicking in the shallows, chasing each other, splashing, throwing seaweed at one another. Jazmina kept a watchful eye as the captain wished he was on a stakeout.

Casually, he glanced around at the mixture of turistas and locals. All was peaceful apart for the gathering of people and his niños and esposa making their way over to it. He stood, stretched, and then started over. Probably a dead shark, he thought. It was Fabiola's scream that pushed Captain Mondragon into a full run.

"¡Ceder el paso! Ceder el paso! Policía!" he shouted as she shoved people out of the way. Everyone was in a circle and people were muttering about how crime is everywhere; what would Sanderson think if he saw this and how could something like this happen here in paradise?

The captain stopped when he saw the mess of limbs, hair, blood, sand, torn clothes, and seaweed. "Don't touch it." He barked orders on a regular basis and it came naturally to him.

The crowd froze and he took a stick from a slack-jawed gringo and began to flick away the seaweed and other flotsam. As more and more flesh was revealed, his eyes grew wide. "I need a phone.

Now!"

Christine's face was bruised and there was a large gash across her face. Her arms and legs were entwined with the bloated, pink, veiny corpse of the late Juan de Dios. There were crabs feasting from the stiletto holes on the chest.

A young boy poked the body and giggled as the crabs scattered. Captain Mondragon found a phone and was barking orders. The boy again poked, this time Christine.

He screamed when a hand latched onto his leg and the eyes fluttered open. "Ayuda!"

The captain turned and nearly screamed himself as the boy was being attacked by what he had supposed to be a dead body. It had latched onto the ankle and was tearing at the flesh. The crowd screamed and started to flee. The young boy was screaming and crying.

Captain Mondragon leapt into action. A swift kick to the man's face collapsed the nose and it let go. He threw the boy to the ground who was instantly scooped up into the arms of his terrified mother.

The captain had no time to worry about the wailing child. He needed to stop this seemingly undead monster from attacking anymore of his people.

The creature was crawling across the sand, dragging its bloodied stumps. Pieces of bone and sinew glistened in the sun. *Probably got caught in the propellers*, Mondragon thought as he pushed people out of the way. In the back of his mind, he knew there was something else he had to worry about, something more important. But, for the life of him, he had no idea.

Then he heard the scream.

Little Fabiola was crying and trying to punch at the mouth tearing at her stomach. Juanito cradled her head while their madre tried with all her might to pull the monster off her darling daughter. Everyone was screaming and a couple of turistas were busy taking photos and videos. Captain Mondragon was frozen, his legs refusing to move.

Finally, Jazmina managed to tear the horror away from her niña. Unfortunately, the jaws were strong and had snapped down like a bear trap. They ended up ripping out the poor little girl's stomach, kidney, and a part of her intestines. Blood spewed forth from Fabiola's mouth and it pulsed and squirted from the hole in her body. She began to tremble and spasms coursed through her body as both the Captain and Jazmina cried out, "¡Por Dios, ayuda!"

#

"¡Ayuda!" Christine shouted as her arms flailed about. It took a moment for her to become orientated but as soon as her eyes focused, her heart sank. Scanning her surroundings, she found herself in an old hospital room. Obviously, the entire building was old. A sharp throbbing pain in her forehead snapped back her attention. Gingerly, she reached up and touched the spot. Christine winced and decided to leave it alone. She laid back and closed her eyes, forcing herself to put order in her mind.

The scream startled her. It was animalistic with the hint of a human voice. *For fuck sakes*, Christine thought as she sat up once again. She swung her feet across the bed and put them on the floor. Immediately, she regretted doing so. When she looked down, she cursed her own bad luck.

Her feet were right in the middle of a large cold sticky pool of blood. Floating in it was fragments of bone, bits of tissue, and what appeared to be skin. Any other day, Christine would have thought torture or an incursion gone wrong. Now? One word. Zombie.

Move, her mind screamed.

Christine leapt over the blood straight for the door. Pulling and bashing the wood did nothing. It had been locked and barricaded.

"Ayuda," she screamed, hoping that an orderly, nurse, or even a doctor would hear her. A splintering scream greeted her ear excitedly as she pressed it to the door. Christine ignored the pain and listened.

The whir of the air-conditioner, the hum of the P.A; usual hospital sounds. She couldn't hear people though. And what had caused that scream?

Christine banged on the door again and then waited.

There! A shuffling sound. Definitely feet.

Another set joined the first. Christine couldn't control her smile. Someone was coming!

A third set appeared. And another. And another. Soon, there was more than ten sets of shuffling shambling feet. The smile faded from Christine's face when she heard it: heavy wheezing breathing mixed with sighs, moans, and groans.

The door shuddered and buckled from the group slamming against it. Christine backed away from the old wood as another hit caused it to splinter.

Looking around, she couldn't see her clothes. *Fucking fantastic*, she thought. Another hit and the hinges moaned. Soon, the horde would be in and Christine gone.

Christine's eyes darted about the room, looking, searching for an escape. There were the windows. *No*, she thought. *If I slip and fall, I'll be lunch.* She then checked the ventilation grates. They were old and slightly rusted. The last time they had been changed must've been well over three decades. The two grates were small and extremely well fixed to the walls. The bolts were heavy duty, industrial if Christine had to guess.

The door bent inward as the group of zombies pressed against it. Its wood began to crack and drop to the floor. The moans from the monsters filled the room, echoing off the tiled walls. Christine had to act fast.

She grabbed the IV stand that had been trailing her and yanked the needle from out her arm. Christine winced but kept moving. She needed to move.

Over by the window, Christine picked up the stand and swung as hard as she could.

The glass cracked and spider legs ran across the pane. She had no time and swung again.

As the metal stand shattered the glass, the door gave up and collapsed. The wood shattered under the weight of the undead who tumbled and fell into a writhing pile. Christine spun. *Fuck me sideways*, ran through her mind. She readied herself, holding the metal IV stand so that she could defend or attack as needed.

Slowly, the monsters untangled themselves, grappling at each other as they clambered back to their feet. Christine braced herself for the onslaught. She didn't have to wait for long.

Her feet slid slightly as a couple of the zombies barreled into her. The IV stand was the perfect barrier as Christine could push on it easily. Each push shoved the mass of the undead back. They wouldn't stay there long. As they ran back at her and collided with the stand, Christine was losing her footing, slowly being forced back, back towards the shattered glass and the drop.

Christine was covered in sweat as she forced the horde back and back. Her knuckles were white and bloodied from scratches and claws. She had to force herself not to gag from the rancid smell. "You guys need to have a bath," she growled as her feet touched the tiled wall. Christine cried out as a shard of glass sliced her back.

Quickly, she glanced out the window. There was a ledge that seemed to go all along the perimeter of the building. Finally, an escape route! Christine breathed heavily and braced herself.

With an almighty throw, the zombies fell backwards. Christine used the moment to break the rest of the jagged pieces of glass and then she jumped out the window, landing on the balls of her feet on the concrete ledge. Pressing herself flat against the brick wall, Christine breathed in a sigh of relief. The air was wonderful and the slight breeze was refreshing on her flesh.

A clammy hand grabbed her ankle and tugged. Christine gasped and tried to pull herself free. The zombie snarled at her and the other arm shot out, trying to reach her. Christine pummeled the squishy dead flesh and it collapsed in on itself, the bone having become spongy. Her eyes caught sight of a phone in an arm holder. Before this, this guy was probably a jogger.

Thinking quickly, Christine dropped forward while spinning, the force of her action ripping the arm from its socket. Blood spurted over the ledge and down onto the cement below. Christine grabbed the ledge with one arm while using the other to pull the zombie forward. She held onto the arm with the phone and as the zombie passed her legs, she kicked at the shoulder.

There was a sickly crunch followed by a squelch and the zombie fell. It hit the ground and exploded, sending organs, fluids, blood, and bone flying across the ground.

Christine shimmied across the ledge and then when she felt the coast was clear, clambered back up. Her arms were tired and screamed at her; both knees were scrapped, but they would be fine.

Carefully, she removed the phone and tossed the severed arm down to the ground. She quickly dialed. "It's me. This is an unsecured line. Put me through to the old man... Just do it!"

She waited for the tell-tale static that preceded the click.

"This better be important."

"Station Master! The situation is fucked-up beyond all recognition!"

"No situation is ever completely FUBAR'ed."

"You've never seen anything like this." Christine started to slowly shimmy across the ledge, being careful to not slip on or in anything. The fall would kill her if she took a misstep.

"Zombies."

Christine was surprised by the one-word response. "You know about it?"

There was a slight chuckle from the old man. "It's on the news. Everyone is reporting about how Cuba has fallen to a plague. Satellite photos show some parts of the island are ablaze... Christine, what is happening with the mission?"

"The Mission? Station Master the mission is over. Cuba is gone, completely overrun with fucking zombies! Do you expect me to continue the damn mission?" She was breathing hard and a part of her wanted to reach through the phone and throttle the old man.

"And?" Station Master said. "What has that go to do with stopping you?"

"You are an old blind fool," she bellowed into the phone. As she passed a window, she glanced inside. There were more zombies shambling about; men, women, and little children zombies. The children were casually gnawing on flesh. "I don't know if Sanderson is still alive. Right now, I'm trapped in a hospital! Is there an EVAC for me?"

There was another silence and Christine thought that it would be better to hang up and take care of everything herself. "I'm on my way to Havana. Do not do anything until you see me. Understand?"

"Yes, sir, but what about President Sanderson?"

"Find someplace safe, Christine. We'll take care of the president together." Before she could answer, the phone clicked.

Christine kept moving along the ledge until she came to the corner.

"Christine?" Signal's voice was shaky.

"What is it? Is everything okay?" She peered around the edge and wanted to scream: Fuck you Cuba! The ledge was demolished. Below her was a van. Maybe, if she was really lucky, the fall would not kill her, just knock her about a little. And then, maybe the keys were in the ignition.

"I got that translation done. You are not going to believe this."

As Signal's voice fought through the static, Christine could not comprehend what she was hearing. The information changed everything and finally gave her the upper hand.

"You haven't shown anyone else? Told no one?" Christine asked when Signal had finished.

"What do you think I am? A fucking novice? The information has already been destroyed."

"Good."

"Be careful," Signal said. "This has gotten more dangerous."

"You fucking think?" Christine was lining up the jump to the van. "I'll be fine. See you on the other side," Christine said then she opened the back of the phone and took the SIM card out. She snapped it in her fingers and then tossed the remains to the winds.

"Right," she said as she jumped.

#

Havana was pandemonium. The zombies were everywhere, tearing people apart, feasting on the flesh, and savoring the sweet tastes. Some of the buildings were burning. Whatever had happened during the short period of time Christine had spent at the hospital, it had created a clusterfuck.

The van had started easily and as Christine drove it through the carpark and onto the main road, she had had the satisfaction of running over the undead. The heads popped off and exploded easily. Now she was putting pedal to the metal and racing through the streets of Havana with one thought on her mind, *Please don't let Sanderson be dead or a zombie.* She tried to imagine the reaction to a zombie president…the end of the world as everyone knew it. As she ran down a pack of the decaying monsters, Christine wondered, *Maybe this IS the end.*

Hopefully, the President of the United States was safe in a bunker or on his way back to the USA. If not? Then he would probably be still at the Saratoga and that would Christine's last chance to… *JESUS FUCKING CHRIST!*

The van swerved, missing a small cat that was fleeing some children zombies. The vehicle careened down the street and through a pool of blood. The wheels, now slick from the thick liquid, spun out. Christine lost control of the van and it spun.

It hit a concrete barrier and flipped. Christine braced herself for the hard impact and hoped that if the car rolled that her safety restraints would hold.

As the van rolled and slid, Christine could hear and see zombies being crushed, smashed, wiped across the cement and decimated by the heavy metal vehicle. Christine tried to make herself go limp, as she was told to do in training for being tense resulted in a greater chance of broken bones. Loose and limp? About half; odds she gladly took right now.

A brick wall stopped the van. The metal chassis bent around the corner, almost snapping in two. Inside, Christine was stunned, not sure what the fuck had just happened, but thankful anyway for whatever was looking out for her. She undid the seatbelt and covered her head as she landed.

Now right-side-up, she looked out the cracked windshield and smiled at what she saw.

The Saratoga didn't look like a hotel anymore. Now it had the appearance of a military bunker with the full might of USA paranoia on full display. Sandbags piled high with barb wire on top and a .50 Cal machine gun inside. The roof had hastily erected sentry stations. Each one had a large searchlight, sniper rifle, and what looked like an RPG. On either side of the steps leading up to the main entrance stood a mix of CIA agents and Cuban military. Surrounding the old hotel was a convoy of black SUVs and military jeeps with more .50 caliber machine guns mounted.

Christine knew there was no way on Earth she would be getting up to the President's suite. Time was running out for both them all and she knew she had this last chance before the end of the festival. As she scrambled out of the wrecked fan, a flurry of movement caught her eye.

A group of thirty-ish zombies were making their shambling way towards the Saratoga. Along the barricades and on the roof, men in suits and army fatigues ran and quickly assumed their positions. *CIA and Cuban army*, Christine thought as she watched the large caliber weapons unleash a rain of death upon the undead. The heavy-duty bullets tore through the tattered stained clothes, ripping the flesh and rendering it a pulpy mess.

Some of the CIA agents whooped and hollered joyously at the sight of the violence. Christine shook her head as did the Cubans. *Fucking cowboys*, she thought as the zombies that were able to scattered. Some of the stragglers and wounded kept on moving towards the hotel. They were almost on the steps.

The shots from the sniper rifles rang out, echoing and startling Christine slightly. The crack-shots were quick and used one bullet for each zombie.

A scream made Christine spin, her arms reaching for a weapon she did not have. A family of tourists were trying to escape from a small group of zombies. They were fat and dressed like gringo turistas. The fat child was having the most trouble running from the monsters. As Christine watched them trip and get devoured, her eyes scanned the area.

Christine Moore hadn't noticed it earlier, but there were more scenes of turistas being bitten, ripped into, and getting fucked up by the zombies. Her nose then caught the smell of burning and she realized that some people must've taken it upon themselves to burn the undead. Havana was more and more becoming like a zombie movie. And not the fun kind.

Looking back to the Saratoga, Christine smiled. Sanderson was being escorted by the CIA agents and surrounding them were the Cuban Military. They all carried AK-47s and swept the area with their eyes while using the barrel sights to keep aim. As they took each step towards the convoy of cars, Sanderson cowered. Christine allowed herself a smile at that then her eyes locked onto her target.

From the side streets next to the hotel, the zombies emerged. They looked fresher than the others Christine had seen. They moved a little quicker and seemed to know what they were doing. They swarmed towards the escort and Sanderson screamed. The

AKs roared and spat fire. The zombies hit the concrete steps in pools of blood. The group of men stopped and smiled. They had done their jobs well... Fuck!

The zombies started to crawl and pull themselves towards the men again. Sanderson bolted down towards the SUVs which were all massive and black with tinted windows. They screamed Presidential and one of the middle ones had its doors open. The agents and soldiers started firing again. Only this time, they were aiming for the heads. Put the fuckers down for good they seemed to chant. Christine saw her opportunity.

President Aaron Sanderson dodged the zombies while cowering and dived headfirst into the waiting SUV. "Go! Go! Go! Go!"

"Mister President," Christine said the moment the doors locked, which she knew to be standard procedure in hostile territory, "you MUST listen to me. Whatever your—"

"Fuck me!" the leader of the free world was panicking. "Whatever you want, I'll give you! Money! Power! Anything! Just fucking drive!" He was crying now, sobbing, and all former traces of control and power had vanished. All that was left was a child crying for his mommy.

"President Sanderson, you don't understand. Your life will end today if you stay in Cuba."

"No fucking shit!"

Christine tried to remain calm, but seeing a president act like this it was hard. There was banging and shouting on the doors. The CIA agents were screaming for the president to unlock the doors. Christine didn't have much time.

She turned to the President. "You need to leave now. Or at least get to somewhere safe."

"That's what I'm trying to do, you bitch!" Sanderson was beginning to calm down. Having his men nearby helped. He was sliding away from Christine, moving towards the door.

"I know, Mister President, but you need to understand something. You cannot trust anyone. Not the Cubans, not even your own men."

The banging and shouting was now being mixed with gunshots. Outside, they could make out the rapid muzzle flashes of the automatic weapons firing.

"Fuck that! Why should I believe you?"

Without thinking, Christine said, "You heard of The Station?"

CHAPTER TWENTY

Christine had been in many prisons over her career with the Station. The ones she remembered the most vividly were Siberia, Afghanistan, Bali, and Mexico. Each one had something about it that made it unbearable and the prisoner willing, almost eager, to talk just so there was a chance to be killed or moved. That was the beauty of these prisons. They didn't need elaborate torture devices or thousands of mean guards. No. Just let the walls and climate do the job. Except for Mexico; there they had full little cities inside the prison with its own economy and way of life. That was certainly memorable, but now she could add Cuban to her list.

Christine had been dragged from the SUV by the CIA. Sanderson had managed to unlock the door and at that moment, the world came crashing down on top of her. She was thrown to the ground and had landed in a puddle of blood. She wanted to gag but the knee pressing down on her back stopped her. A black felt bag was slipped over onto her head and all she could do was listen.

Amidst the occasional AK or sniper rifle going off, Christine could hear a heated debate happening between the CIA and Cubans. The Americans wanted to take her off island to a facility for extraordinary rendition, but the Cubans countered that with the fact since she had landed the plague had come. Both were getting ready to fight when Sanderson stepped in. "Gentlemen, we can and must work together. Right now, our only concern should be safety. So might I suggest we get the fuck outta here!"

Now here she was, sitting on an ancient bunk that had never seen better days. The walls were old and caked in mud and moss.

There was graffiti on the walls and when she had read them, her stomach turned somersaults. There was mention of Theodore Roosevelt and his Roughriders; another dealing with Batista and Castro. She swallowed then shuddered when she saw the toilet. At least she hoped it was. In one corner, some industrious felon had managed to chisel and crack away at the cement floor until there was nothing but a small hole. The rancid smell told her that this was the facilities.

From outside, she could hear screams, sirens, gunfire, and general pandemonium. A loud PA message was being repeated over and over. Unfortunately, the power was failing and she could only hear every other word. But the gist of it was, "Stay inside. Do not go out. If anyone in your house is sick, then get them out of the house ASAP."

Christine started to pace the cell. She had been in this situation before, but there was always a distraction. The cold in Siberia; the flies in Bali; the city in Mexico. But here? Nothing. Absolutely nothing except her own mind, and the apocalypse happening outside. Apart from that, she didn't know how long she had been in this cell. There were no windows.

A thought started to form in the back of her mind. *Is it really worth it? After all that has happened to you, why not give up?* The thought continued to spread and as it did memories of all her past failures started to fade into view.

Rafael's dead body, the eyes staring unblinking at her; the face frozen forever in uncomprehending horror and shock. How could she have let him die? Then she saw Juan, his bloated body bobbing up and down in the Bay. He seemed to beckon her towards him, but that would mean giving up. Christine could not do that, never would. The mission was always first. Nothing came second.

Adriana. The name whispered itself and Christine frowned. She was the cause of everything shitty to ever have happened to her. Christine started to count backwards all the ways Adriana had hurt her.

The most recent was lying to her about Jeremiah Banks and working for the government. Christine could forgive the lie about the government. After all that was her job: to lie and steal secrets for the Cubans in whatever manner she deemed fit.

Used to be her job, Christine reminded herself. *Used to be.* But then how long had Adriana been actually working for Jeremiah Banks? Apart from that remark from Juan about recruiting her, Christine actually knew very little about the woman who professed her love.

Christine snorted. Love. Had they ever really had that? Even back five years ago, it had seemed so. But when Christine started to think about the way it was, she knew that Adriana had played her perfectly.

The night she asked Christine to give her information came just after they had told each other that they loved them. Then they had made their way to La Bodeguita and while dancing Adriana whispered, "I need your help, Chris." Christine, naturally, offered to do anything. "No, not this. Forget I had ever asked." Adriana then kept the subject light the rest of the night.

Days had gone by and all was fine between them. The sex was intense, the missions daring and dangerous, and their nights at dinner romantic and perfect. Then one day, Adriana arrived at the Nacional with bruises and cigar burns on her body. "The most dangerous man in the world did this to me, as punishment for not getting something."

Christine begged her to tell her everything, that she wouldn't be angry or hate her and that their life together was more important than sides. Adriana smiled and said. "Thank you, mi vida, pero you cannot help me. No matter how much I want it, this is something you will never do."

The sadness in her voice broke Christine's heart and she said, "I will do anything for you."

"En serio?" Adriana replied. "Then what this man, this terrible plague on the planet wants is the names of all Station agents in Cuba."

Christine had shaken her head at that and walked away. For almost a week, neither had said anything to the other and her life was duller, but the job was easier without the distraction. During that period, Christine had grown worried and had started to make an investigation into this terrible man. That was before she had gotten the call.

Adriana had been raped and left for dead. Christine had the address of the hospital and raced over the moment she had gotten the news. She was in intensive care and fighting for her life. The doctors didn't think she was going to last the night. The next morning, Adriana opened her eyes and smiled at the sleeping Christine. They spoke soon and apologized for being idiots and then Christine asked who had done it.

Adriana said one name and Christine knew what she must do. "Don't worry about Jeremiah Banks," she had said. "I've been tracking him. Soon, he is going to die. I promise."

But the Cuban shook her head. "If he dies, then I die. Christine! There is only one way for him to leave me, us, alone. Give him the names."

Again, Christine repeated that she could not do that but caved after Adriana said, "He promised that the next time he found me, all that would be found would be my…nipples. He said those because you out of all the people in Cuba would know them."

Christine took a day before giving Adriana the names and getting a promise that after this they would be left alone. She was a fool for believing the lies.

The ten other agents were found and then publicly executed by a Haitian Death Squad. A note was left on the bodies saying that if anyone touched them, they would meet the same fate.

Three days had passed before the people started to scavenge the bodies, taking the wallets and money first, then the clothes, and finally leaving the naked rotting corpses for the birds and dogs.

Christine was exiled and threatened with death by Station Master and sent to Siberia. For two years, she was locked away, fighting for her life every day, until she got the call to go to the Alps and pick up a delivery.

And now here she was, in Havana again, and having to worry about not only an assassination but also the fucking end of the world. *If this gets off the island and to either Mexico or the USA, how long until the world is gone?* The question floated in her mind until she realized that all her problems had come from one place and one person.

"Station Master!" She cursed the name with every ounce of loathing and hatred she could muster.

"What have I done," an old voice asked.

#

Station Master sat there in his wheelchair, a light tan suit on and in his lap a floppy panama hat. He looked distinctively odd compared to all the other times Christine had seen him, always in a black or dark gray suit, sometimes a cardigan on top and never a hat. "What have I done to deserve that kind of hatred?"

Christine leapt to her feet and ran to the bars. "You," she exclaimed. "You have been at the heart of all my problems."

Station Master chuckled. "Just like my own daughters," he said. "Always blaming me for their own actions. Let me tell you something, Miss Moore. If I wanted it, you would still be rotting away in that Siberian prison, remember? That was the consequences for your own actions. That is what life is: action and reaction. You do something and there are consequences. Never forget that!" His breathing was labored and he gripped the armrests of his chair.

"Then why are you here? You've always played it safe. We fuck up and you throw us under the bus."

"Don't act like such a child," Station Master reprimanded her. "Now, give me the SITREP."

Christine blinked. What was he doing here? Instead of asking that, she said, "Fucked beyond all recognition. You must've have seen it?"

The old man nodded and looked up at the roof. "From above, like a god I did. Christine, what has happened here?"

"Station Master? We don't have time for this! We have to save Sanderson! That's the mission now. Please!"

A chuckle escaped the ancient mouth. "You don't dictate the mission. I do. Never forget that. Now, report!"

The tone snapped Christine's training into action. "Somehow the dead have risen. Zombies. They have taken the island, sir. Unless we get out now, our chances are slim to none. As for the original mission, Jeremiah Banks is a lunatic who believes he is a revolutionary. He will stop at nothing to get what he wants. I believe that maybe he is responsible somehow for this outbreak." That last part made her blink. "Station Master, I have to get out of here. President Sanderson is in danger. He just got off the island."

The old iron cell door screeched open. Station Master was beside the controls and he smiled. "The mission has changed, Christine. Are you ready?"

Even though she was far from ready, her body screaming at her to stop and rest, her mind at the breaking point, Christine Moore nodded. Station Master smiled. "Good. You need to find Jeremiah Banks. He is of vital importance"

"Why?"

"You said it yourself, 'He maybe is responsible for this.' NATO and my contacts in the USA agree; they think he is or knows who has caused this. We need him alive. He has vital information. Get him back to the Station House, alive. Understood?"

There was a large explosion outside that caused the building to shake and dust fell from the roof. Christine looked around, checking to see if there were any cracks or structural damage. Station Master checked his watch and shook his head. "That can't have been them. I was guaranteed another three hours."

"Who guaranteed what and why?"

She watched as the old man casually wiped from sweat away from his face. It was the first time she could remember seeing him do this. "Station Master?"

He sighed. "Presidente Esposito has given his clearance and NATO has accepted it that in light of the bio-hazard that has hit Cuba, the mortality rate and the unknown source and way to cure it… Cuba is going to be bombed; a mixture of Thermite and Napalm. In about three hours, the jets will deliver the payload and wipe the slate clean. You have that time to not only capture Jeremiah Banks and get him off the island, but also you have to save President Sanderson."

"Really? Fuck?"

Station Master nodded. "You may be right about Sanderson being in danger. Do you know where he's getting picked up from?"

Christine shook her head; of course she didn't know. Station Master knew this too and loved the power of knowledge. "La Cabaña. But here's the thing, Christine, there may be a mole in his protection. We have reasons to believe that the head of his CIA detail, an Agent Harris, is working for Banks. Sanderson's EVAC is happening at La Cabaña, but there is the high chance that it is a trap set up by Banks. So—"

"I need to get Sanderson to change his EVAC location and then find Banks. And then get the fuck out of Dodge. All within three hours. Easy."

"Glad to see you think so," Station Master said with a slight smile.

Christine smiled as she stepped out of the cell. "How long have I got?"

Station Master flicked his head to the door. "You better move."

#

The sun was shining brightly and it nearly blinded her. It took a moment for Christine's eyes to readjust to the light after the dingy darkness of the jail cell. Looking around, Christine saw the cause of the explosion. A petrol tanker had smashed into a building and exploded. Her eyes locked onto La Cabaña and she smiled. It was close, maybe two kilometers; an easy walk normally, but who knew how many of the undead she would find.

A buzzing made her look up and she saw the helicopter hovering expertly while a two-man team waited with safety lines. One saluted her while the other constantly looked about, worried. "Sanderson first, Miss Moore," Station Master said as he rolled over to the two men. Quickly, they set about connecting the chair to the lines and secured him. Then they connected themselves and waited as a third man above them activated the winch and slowly they rose into the air.

"How do I find Sanderson?" Christine called.

"With this." A small GPS dropped from the helicopter right into Christine's open hands. "And that."

Christine followed the finger and smiled.

CHAPTER TWENTY-ONE

All 14.5 tonnes of the BTR-50 APC crashed through the abandoned apartment block. The bricks, mortar, and rebar did very little to slow the vehicle down. Inside, Christine was enjoying herself immensely as she used the six large wheels to crush the undead that came between her and Sanderson's convoy.

Glancing down periodically at the GPS, she saw that she was getting closer to her target. All she had to do was figure out a way to stop them without causing any injuries. *Why not go and handle this yourself*, she thought, imagining Station Master sitting next to her. *The President is more likely to believe you than me.* Christine fought a giggle as she remembered their first encounter. *How to win friends*, she mused as she spun the wheel to the right. She didn't know which street she was on. It didn't really matter though. All she had to do was force the convoy to stop. Easy enough when you're driving an armored personnel carrier.

Another fifty meters and she would have caught up with them. The GPS showed a T-intersection coming and Christine had an idea.

The speedometer read 35kms; not nearly fast enough. Christine shifted into fourth gear and punched it. The heavy armor-plated vehicle surged forward, roaring as it hit the maximum speed: 44kms. Silently, Christine hoped that the cold-welded steel plates would hold and not bend inward, impaling herself. She lined up the BTR-50 and braced herself.

.

#

"Fuck me sideways," President Aaron Sanderson could only utter as he watched a small hotel's base exploded and then toppled. The brick, wood, and tiles blocked the path perfectly. His convoy had to swerve and come to a screeching halt. The force of the sudden stop made him drop his cigar in his lap and spill the bourbon he was sipping at.

"Sir, stay in the vehicle," one of the Aviator-wearing CIA agents ordered as the president watched the rest step out of the vehicles and flip the safeties on their weapons to off.

He couldn't believe his fucking luck. A day ago, he was lounging about in a rooftop swimming pool with the crème de la crème of Cuban pussy, having anyone he wanted and not needing to worry or give a fuck about the language. Then, drinking and smoking as much as he wanted. And all this on the American taxpayer's dime. Fucking heaven. Of course, that was then. After that night when that crazy bitch nearly twisted off his pecker did it all start to go downhill.

First, Esposito started demanding more and more, wanting a guarantee that whatever happened with the negotiations, he would be paid well. *Fucking politicians*, Sanderson always thought. Next, they get reports that there are fucking zombies sweeping across the island. Fucking zombies! All the agents say they need to EVAC ASAP, but the boys back in D.C. nix the idea; not news friendly for the president to run away.

Since then, he's seen all different kinds of shit and just wants to go back to Nevada. But, here he is, watching a country crumble and tear itself to pieces. Literally.

"You have got to be fucking kidding," he exclaims, eyes going wide and his mind not comprehending. Before his mind knows what is happening, President Aaron Sanderson is out of the safety of his vehicle, walking over to the wreckage and shouting, "You should be in fucking jail!"

The CIA agents all had their weapons, Beretta handguns, Glocks, a couple had small Uzis and one had an AK he had gotten from a Cuban, pointed at Christine who was casually climbing out of the BTR-50. A smile on her face and a casual gait to her walk,

Christine Moore looked calm, cool, and collected as she sauntered up to the president. "Sorry, I didn't quite hear that."

The agents didn't know what to do as their commander-in-chief stood dumbstruck. "You. Should. Be. In. Fucking. Jail," he finally managed to spit out. His face looked as if he had been slapped with a large black cock and been told that was dinner.

"You need to listen," Christine began, not giving a shit about the agents, their weapons, or the powerful man before her. "You are heading to a trap. Whoever told you that La Cabaña was safe is setting you up to be eaten."

"Eaten," one of the agents scoffed. The rest laughed but were silenced by Christine's look. She did just after all collapse a hotel on their asses.

"Yes, fucking eaten." She turned to Sanderson. "Do you wanna live? Go back to fucking your way through the interns?"

Sanderson nodded slowly, his mind trying to find the logic in this situation. Only one thing came to his mind. "Why should I trust you?"

A scream from one of the men made him jump. The rest turned, weapons going up and they forgot how to fire. The poor soul was being munched on by a small horde of zombie children. They had come up from the wreckage and gone for the first man. His legs buckled as they bit and clawed at the knees and ankles. The moment he fell, it would be game over.

"Open fire," Christine barked, shocking the rest of the entourage into action. The bullets teared and shredded the small dead flesh to pieces and the zombified children died gasping. The agent collapsed but quickly started to snarl and crawl towards them.

"Jesus Christ," Sanderson exclaimed, sidling up next to Christine for protection.

They're changing faster, she thought and hoped that more would not show up.

"Sweet fancy Moses."

From out of the abandoned buildings—well to Christine they looked abandoned but then this is Havana—the undead shambled shuffled and crawled out and onto the street; men, women, and children all at various stages of decay. The children looked the worst for in life they had been malnourished and mostly skeletal, but in death, the skin had stretched across the faces, pulling up at the cheekbones, making them appear as if they had a permanent grin. Those without facial wounds, that is. Most had been attacked and lost chunks of flesh, pieces of ears, limbs, and other body parts, making the herd a dangerous disgusting Picasso.

Christine felt something clammy clap itself to her arm. Her hand sprang up automatically and she had to fore herself not to break Sanderson's hand. He was pale and sweat poured off him. For an instant, Christine felt sorry for the man, being in a situation that nobody on Earth had training for. Then just as quickly she realized that was everyone stuck in Cuba. *Fucking cretin*, she thought, slapping the hand away.

The zombies started snarling, arms raised, and it seemed as if they were already reaching out to the small group. It was odd to Christine that they didn't move at the same pace. The children, younger and fresher-looking ones, moved slightly faster than the older and more decayed monsters.

A growl behind them caused the frightened president to cry out, standing on top of the rubble that had been a hotel was a pack of dogs. At least that is what they should have been. Some were missing legs, others tails, a couple had fought either other dogs or people and lost. They were snarling, salivating, and eyeballing the tasty treats waiting for them.

Christine's eyes went from the pack back to the herd and then to the undead agent that was slowly crawling towards them.

"What do we do?"

Sanderson was tugging on her shoulder. "What do we do?"

She glared at the man, shutting him up as her mind worked overtime. A thought started to form when the dogs barked and lunged. The five hell hounds made a beeline for the first couple of agents who instinctively opened fire. Fingers squeezing the triggers, Sanderson flinched as the bullets erupted forth.

"Keep firing," Christine bellowed as she grabbed the terrified president by the scruff of his neck. She yanked him and they started to run.

"Take the fuckers down," Sanderson screamed, trying with all his might to sound authoritative. Unfortunately, the girlish whimpering ruined it. But his men, all loyal and good soldiers, obeyed. They formed two protective lines, one in front of Christine and Sanderson, taking care of the dogs while the rest brought up the rear.

"Where to, ma'am?"

Christine pointed with her head. "To my car."

As one complete unit, they started to move. The zombie dogs didn't put up much of a fight to the training of the CIA. Behind them, the rearguard would do short bursts of gunfire when the zombies got too close. Christine had her eyes on the BTR-50 which she was positive would still be able to get their sorry asses out of there.

"To the left, the door is open. Sweep it first then give me the all clear," Christine barked the orders with the same tone as a drill sergeant. The men around her snapped to attention and the front line moved quickly.

Christine pulled Sanderson up and stared into his panicking eyes. "The moment you get in, move to the front and strap yourself in... I can't believe I'm saying this... You are too important to die here."

President Aaron Sanderson smiled his best charming smile. "You warming up to me?" Before Christine could answer, he grabbed her and planted his lips upon hers. He moaned slightly while she silently screamed. Meanwhile, the CIA agents moved into the APC, then quickly came out, but when they saw the president locking lips, they averted their eyes. "All clear," one muttered as the rear guard continued their burst firing.

Christine heard the agent and did the only thing she could think of to end this impromptu make-out session. She grabbed one of his ears and quickly twisted it while pulling on it sharply.

The US President squealed and his men tried not to laugh. Christine looked at the closet man. "This belongs to you." She held out the president who was trying not to cry since his ear was now becoming bright red.

"Thanks, ma'am."

Christine walked past the men and straight into the APC. "Move it!"

#

It hadn't taken long for the CIA agents to contact their HELO and change the EVAC location. While they had done this, Christine got the BTR-50 in motion, crushing all of the zombies that were in their way. Sanderson sat sullenly, rubbing his ear and glaring at the woman who handled the controls better than most professional tank drivers. She ignored all attempts at conversation, her mind seemingly somewhere else.

"ETA?"

"Another ten minutes," an agent said. "It's near the original site. About three blocks away; intel says it's clear and stable. No bogies caught by the done."

Christine nodded. "Here. Punch in the coordinates."

The location was in Old Havana, and as the agent said, was stable. By the time they had arrived, a Black Hawk helicopter was already hovering, waiting for its precious payload. Christine didn't wait for the goodbyes as each man ran to the building. Only Sanderson tried to say some words. He opened his mouth but was surprised when Christine slammed the door shut and the President of the United States of America was covered in dust as the large, heavy vehicle sped away.

As Christine steered the BTR, she tried to picture what was waiting for her at La Cabaña. Zombies probably. Jeremiah Banks? Definitely. Adriana? If she saw that traitorous bitch, what would she do? *No fucking clue*, she chuckled to herself.

The old fortress was coming in to view quickly. Christine checked her watch; another hour and a half before the fireworks started. *Move your ass*, she told herself. Her feet pressed the clutch and accelerator and the BTR-50 sped up.

She was getting close now and could make out the shambling forms of the undead. The roads, streets, and parks were covered with them. *Cuba is truly lost*, she thought sadly. A part of her was screaming to stop at the gate and not to barrel through it, which was her plan. Her training agreed, as it was folly to barge into a situation without any intel. *That's how you get killed*, she scolded herself.

An explosion shook the APC and for a moment, Christine lost control, the steering wheel slipping from her grip. She heard metal grinding and a display showed that one of the wheels had been destroyed. As Christine fought with the wheel, another explosion almost flipped the vehicle.

"Fuck," Christine bellowed as she slammed both feet down onto the brake, her hands pulling up hard on the handbrake. The sudden drop in speed caused the gears to lock and the engine stalled. But with the weight and inertia kicking in, Christine's BTR-50 kept moving. Straight for a row of metal spikes and right behind that was a metal pole that had been fixed into the ground. Christine braced herself and slammed her eyes shut.

CHAPTER TWENTY-TWO

Coughing and spluttering, Christine pulled herself from the smoking wreckage. She rolled onto her back and tried to ignore all the aches and pains that had invaded her body. Slowly, she took three deep breaths, exhaling after each one. That helped. Her heartbeat had started to slow. How long had she been out? Christine didn't know, so gently she raised her hand and glanced at the watch.

The face was completely destroyed; most likely during the crash, she had been thrown around and at some point, a control panel had gotten in the way. Christine laughed.

"¿Qué es tan jodiamente gracioso?" a familiar voice grunted. Christine rolled and then scrambled to her feet, a small smile threatening to become bigger.

Adriana Prado was knee-deep in a river of the undead. In her hands, she wielded two large, old, and extremely mean-looking machetes. They had definitely been looked after over the years because it didn't take much effort for the blades to cut, slice, and dice their way through flesh and bone.

Christine watched and couldn't help but admire the way the Cuban's muscles would tense and bunch up before unleashing a torrent of blows. Adriana's skill with a blade was almost like artwork. "Will you stop eye-fucking me and help!"

Within seconds, the two women were back to back cutting a swath through the horde of the undead towards the large wooden doors of La Cabaña. "What's the plan?"

Adriana ducked then brought one of the blades up, slicing off half the face of a drooling beast. "Get inside!"

Christine nodded; *simple yet effective*. She drove the shard of metal from the wreck into the eye of a zombie. It flinched and took out another two when Christine delivered a roundhouse kick. Quickly, she glanced at the door, her eyes tracing the details, looking for a way in. She ducked and sliced open the face of a zombie. "No idea how to get in!"

Adriana grunted her own reply as one of the machetes became lodged in the skull of a zombie. She spun trying to wrench it free. All she accomplished was to snap the handle and continue into Christine.

Both cried out as they tumbled to the ground. Christine pushed Adriana off her and they both scrambled for the doors. They laid their backs flat against the heavy wood. "Fuck!"

Adriana had to agree; they were running out of time. Christine was covered in cuts and bruises and looked like she was going to pass out soon. "You rest," Adriana said. "We'll take it in turns."

Christine wearily shook her head. "No... No time. Bombing run...soon."

Adriana swore and used her leg to bang on the door. "He better open the fuck up." They both swiped, kicked, and pushed the zombies away, doing their best to keep them at bay. "How long we got?"

"No clue, maybe an hour. Maybe less. Maybe fuck this in the ass!" She ripped the head off a zombie then used it to cave in another's head.

The horde of zombies were closing in; they could smell the strength going from the women. Christine slumped against the door, her body done. Adriana moved, placing herself between the undead gaping maw and her former lover. "I got this."

Christine started to speak but screamed when she lost her footing. The moment she hit the ground, the zombies charged them, snarling, growling, and ready for the feast. It would just be a matter of which one got there first and tasted the flesh.

Adriana clamped her eyes shut from the brightness of the explosion. The zombies in the first couple of rows were instantly vaporised in a mist of deep reds and pale blues. Adriana opened her eyes slightly and traced a fading smoke trail up. She heard a whoosh followed by another explosion. *Missiles or grenade launcher*, she thought. Adriana had to cover her head as more explosions went off. Each one got closer and closer.

Christine looked up. Her eyes grew wide at the bright explosions. A small part of her hoped that something would go wrong and an explosion would go off just that little bit too close. That way she would finally be able to rest. She looked over at Adriana and a new feeling hit her, *Please let us live*!

Something started to move inside all of the destruction. It was crawling on the ground. There was another! And a third! Christine inherently knew what was coming. Zombies!

She was right. Slowly they came, moaning as best they could for the explosions had melted or ripped away flesh, bones, limbs, and organs. Christine and Adriana tried not to gag as the stench of the dead hit their sinuses. Both had never smelled anything like this in their lives, a mixture of putrefied rotting eggs with sulfur and the slightest hint of piss and shit. As the undead got closer and closer, the smell became worse and worse, almost to the point of knocking the women out.

A hand gripped the back of Christine's torn and bloodied shirt and then dragged her backwards into La Cabaña.

#

"You took your damn time," Adriana practically screamed at Jeremiah Banks as he closed the door and bolted the heavy locks. Christine studied the man before her. His suit was extremely dirty and it was obvious that he had had to commit some acts that nearly pushed him over the edge. His eyes were hollow and constantly darting around.

"Let's go," he said as he slung a duffle bag over his shoulder then picked up an older looking sniper rifle with a wooden stock and frames. If Christine had to guess which rifle it was, it would be the Walther WA 2000. *Impressive*, she thought as Adriana helped her up and together they followed Banks towards the tower.

"We don't have much time," Banks was saying. "Pretty soon, President Sanderson will be here and then we can get to work." As they walked, Christine was able to look at La Cabaña properly. It was old, definitely, but over the years since becoming a tourist destination, some modifications and reconstructions had been made. The levels were still obvious even though some had been overgrown with grass and weeds. She looked up at the tower; it had been reinforced and during a past storm, hurricane probably, the roof had been taken off.

"Not long now," Banks was saying with a grin. "Thought you could get away huh? Did Juan de Dios bob back up?" He laughed as his foot kicked open the door at the bottom of the tower.

"Yeah," Christine said quietly. "Caused all the destruction and death you saw out there."

"Wonderful, isn't it?"

"¿Mi país está en ruinas y lo llamas hermoso? ¿Qué mierda te pasa?" Adriana was behind Christine as they climbed the stairs and her tone said it all.

Christine had to agree with her; the situation had gradually been going from bad to worse to completely fucked up. *What next?* she thought as they climbed up and out of a trap door.

It took a moment for her eyes to adjust to the sudden bright light but when they did, she let out a small gasp. Havana was burning. Literally burning. The sky was orange from the flames that had seemingly engulfed the city. Adriana stood next to Christine and fought back her tears. The Capitol Building had been destroyed at some point during the plague. "I was wrong," Christine whispered.

"What was that?" Banks asked as he unloaded the duffle bag. Christine watched as the man took out grenades, lengths of rope, some small rockets for the RPG, and ammo clips for the Walther.

"I was wrong," she said loudly. "The world ends not with a bang, but a whimper."

Jeremiah Banks laughed and clapped his hands. "How fucking philosophical! Of course the world ends like that. It will always end with a whimper. Do you know why?"

Christine shook her head. "Right now, I don't give a fuck. I just want to get off this island."

Banks' eyes darted from Christine to Adriana who was crumpled into a ball of sorrow. "That's why," he said, pointing at the Cuban. "Humans give up so easily. We always will. Always have. But, not me! Even with all of this happening, once that sniveling excuse of president is dead," here he loaded a magazine into the Walther, "the world will be shocked into action. No more whimpering at the darkness. We will go in with lights and blow the fucker up."

"What fucker?"

"Any and all who would stand in the way of my vision!"

Christine started to chuckle. "You think all of this will end in your grand vision for a future world?"

It only took two steps for Banks to be in front of Christine, one hand around her neck, the other holding the sniper rifle inches from her face. "Why don't we wait and see huh? Once Sanderson has a bullet in the brain, let's see how much you're laughing." His eyes were vacant, as if his soul had been ripped out, at least if Christine believed in souls anyway.

"What if he isn't coming?"

Banks blinked, unsure of what he was hearing. "Not coming," he repeated as if in a daze.

Christine Moore nodded. "You heard me. What happens to your grand plan if the key has been locked away somewhere safe...and protected?"

Adriana let out a laugh that was borderline hysterical but quieted down and backed away somewhat when Banks whirled towards her. "You think this funny," he shrieked. "Years of planning ruined. Ruined! By a whore you recommended." The Cuban tripped and fell on her ass while Banks loomed over her. "I should never have listened to you. Albert was right."

There was that name again. Christine had heard it before, but where? She racked her mind, trying to remember but the smells of the sea, burning buildings, and the rotting flesh distracted her. In the distance, a boat signaled. The yacht! *That's his partner*!

"...not my fault if you can't take into account the fucking future," Adriana was explaining as her eyes were focused on the dark foreboding barrel of the Walther. Her hands meanwhile were busy searching for anything she could use as a weapon. "Not to mention that that pendejo told me she would be cooperative. It's his fault!"

Banks' finger twitched slightly as it hovered above the trigger. His mind was working, figuring out the next move. Slowly, Christine started to move towards the forgotten duffle bag. She had her own plan.

"Speaking of Miss Moore," the calm voice froze her. Banks sounded relaxed, as if he was on the yacht again. "You were supposed to escort my partner today and yet…" He looked around. "Where's Albert Bates?"

Christine began to shake her head. "You say that name like it's supposed to mean something.

"¡Espera!… You never knew." Adriana was incredulous. Even Banks couldn't believe what he was hearing. Both started to laugh.

"Care to let me in on the joke," Christine asked, still eyeballing the bag, hoping that they would remain distracted long enough.

Banks shook his head in disbelief. "You poor, poor fool. Albert Bates is your boss. The illustrious Station Master."

Looking between the two, Christine wasn't sure if they were being serious or trying to lure her into a trap. Adriana was trying not to laugh while Banks looked on with barely concealed amusement. "Bullshit," Christine said finally.

Adriana shook her head. "Why do you think you were sent back? Because you paid your dues? Aye por favor!"

"We needed someone who had fucked up already in Cuba. Who better? Originally, we were going to find some young new recruit, but then Albert and the lovely lady here came up with the idea of using you. Genius, really."

"Yeah, fucking stroke of genius," Christine said sullenly, suddenly feeling as if her entire career was one big laughing stock. Then a thought came to her. "Hang on. You said I was supposed to escort him to here?" Banks nodded. "Then why did he send me off while he took a helicopter to safer parts?"

That did it. Jeremiah Banks' eyes flashed and he picked up the RPG and pressed the trigger. A flash of smoke and a whooshing sound then a piece of the wall exploded in a shower of fire and rubble. On the other side of the demolished section, the moans and groans of the zombies could be heard. Banks gently placed the RPG back on the ground then he patted his hair down. "That's better."

Adriana's eyes were on the destroyed wall, the cracks spider-webbing along, and it was obvious that soon the wall would collapse letting in the hordes. "What have you done?"

"There was always a chance that Albert would get cold feet and leave us to fate. No problem." Banks cleared his throat and looked out at the fortress. He reached inside his jacket pocket and pulled out a small square with an antenna and a button. It was smooth and he lovingly rubbed his finger along the sides and surface. "Be prepared, is the saying. Yes? Yes. Not so fast, Miss Moore!"

Christine was kneeling down and just reaching into the bag when the voice stopped her. "Trying to find something to dispose of us with?"

"Or a satellite phone. Whatever I came across first," she replied with a chuckle as she stood. Her eyes zeroed in on the device in the man's hands. "What's that?"

"This…" He held up the device, and Christine knew instantly what it was: a detonator. "This is the back-up plan. What do you think is going to happen to Cuba?"

"I know exactly," Christine said. "They're going to wipe her clean. Napalm. Adios Habana."

Adriana gasped and let out a small childlike, "No." Christine looked at her and nodded; what she said was the truth.

Banks nodded his head. "Standard practices. What next? Years goes by, and then they start to rebuild; probably the Spanish or the Americans. Then a New Cuba in the shape of how they want it to be. I cannot let that happen. So, what happens if the threat is completely wiped out? Would that make them stop? Take a look."

Christine followed Banks over to the edge of the tower and they both looked down. In the water below floating casually was the yacht. Christine glanced to Banks. "My escape route."

"So what do you plan to do with that?"

"Havana has drawn all of the creatures to it. You know why?… No," he chuckled. "A sense memory, if you can call it that. Something makes them come here and soon the entire city will be overrun with them. So this," he waggled the detonator as they went back over to where the stunned Adriana stood, "this, will set off a chain reaction that will cause Havana to collapse into itself, destroying everything. Now, there is a chance that not all will be killed. But over the years, they will starve and die. At which point…"

"At which point you'll come back and rebuild your own little island paradise?"

Banks nodded, impressed with how quickly Christine put it all together. "There needs to be a country like Cuba. Somewhere out of time that is truly a paradise. Now, will this happen overnight? No." He sighed and looked at the gate. "But sacrifices must be made." He clicked the button and the large gate exploded, taking down half of the wall.

"Pendejo!"

Banks turned and let out a small whimper as Adriana tackled him to the ground, the force making him drop the detonator. The two rolled and Adriana ended on top.

She began to throw punch after punch at Banks' face, each hit connecting hard and splitting the skin, crushing bone and smashing teeth. "¡Mi familia!" Squelchy wet slap as her fist landed on Banks' cheek. "¡Mi hogar!" Another; his nose caved in. "¡Mi pais!" She popped his eardrum and blood filled his ear. "Tienes que ayudar!" She split his lips and broke teeth, causing blood to pour from his mouth. "¡Salvanos!" Adriana stopped, panting and looked at her busted knuckles.

Christine stared in awe at the bloody mess that was Jeremiah Banks and also at the zombies pouring into La Cabaña. Slowly, she went over and helped the Cuban up. "Let's get out of here. Cuba is lost."

Adriana shook her off, her face set in stone. She had made a decision and nothing was going to stop her now. Christine watched as Adriana picked up the rope and tied Bank's hands and then his legs. With a couple more ties, he could have been hogtied.

The man started to shake his head and moan as Adriana tied a length to his legs and then dragged him over to the edge. The zombies had smelt the fresh bad and gotten themselves worked up. Christine knew what was coming next but something in her said to let it happen.

Casually, Adriana looped the rope over a metal flagpole that stuck out of the tower. Any second now, she would send Banks to his doom. A messy long doom.

"Adriana, don't," Christine said as she quickly looked up at the sky. Any moment now the jet fighters would be heard and then the fire.

"He must die!"

"But…not…like this," Banks wheezed as he realized what was going to happen. Adriana smiled at him. "Fuck you."

Banks chuckled and kicked. His feet connected with Adriana's chest and as she doubled over, he landed another hard kick that sent her over the edge.

Christine screamed as she watched her lover disappear, the rope tangling around her and unraveling rapidly. She dived for it and as Jeremiah Banks laughed, Christine saw the rope go tight.

Adriana swung out and seemed to float midair. Then gravity kicked in and she smashed into the side of the tower, her face hitting the stone, crumpling in on itself and blood exploding from the ears, mouth, and nose. There was a horrid crack and Adriana Prado was dead.

Christine stared down at the hanging body. Blood drained out of it and poured down, covering the zombies which caused them to get rowdy and reach up. Something in them knew that on top of the tower is where there was more food. If they found the door and got through it, both Banks and Christine were fucked.

"Why are you doing this?" Banks asked as Christine dragged him closer to the edge.

"What? Giving her justice?"

"No," he said with a laugh. "Why are you still following orders? Albert's. The dead whore." He winced as she landed a kick. "The world is coming to an end. Let it happen. We can escape. Survive. Yes?"

Christine stopped, looking at the hanging body, her heart breaking as she realized that Adriana was actually someone she cared for. "Orders are orders," she said.

"Even if they come from a traitorous old devil like him." Banks was beyond surprised. "And what about her? Do you think she truly cared for you? Loved you?"

Christine's eyes went wide as they watched the hanging body twitch, then shudder. With a moan and groan, Adriana's body started to move and she looked up. The black eyes and snarling mouth said it all. Zombified.

"She had a job. To seduce you," Banks was saying, trying to keep himself alive. "Anything and everything she ever told you was a lie… What do you have to say now?"

He watched as she turned, her face expressionless, and deliberately, she dragged him until he was on the very edge. Below, the zombies bellowed as they saw a free meal. Above, the sounds of thunder echoed. *About time*, Christine thought as the sound changed becoming that of jet engines.

Banks shrieked when she kicked him over.

He plummeted down the rope, pulling up the Zombie-Adriana until they were next to each other. Banks whimpered and tried to push her away, but his bound hands made it impossible.

Their motion caused them to swing to and fro; eventually, they would meet. Above, Christine pulled out a piece of shrapnel and waited. Luckily, she didn't have to wait for long.

Adriana smashed into Banks and tore a chunk of his face off. His scream echoed and blood spurted out. He looked up at Christine, "Please!"

Christine Moore shook her head and with one smooth motion, she cut the rope.

Jeremiah Banks plummeted into the zombie abyss as the jet fighters flew over La Cabaña and dropped their payload.

CHAPTER TWENTY-THREE

The news reports all over the world were confusing to say the least. The British were reporting that a remote unknown nuclear power plant had exploded, causing a change reaction that wiped out all life on Cuba. The Asians said that it was an earthquake followed by tsunamis and that it was Gaia returning the balance. It didn't matter; only the UN and the USA knew the truth. Them, and one other man.

Station Master loved Mexico. The people, the cities, the food, the drinks, and the women. He had the money to buy anything and anyone. But the thing he loved most was Acapulco.

He sat on the terrace of the Hotel Mirador restaurant and waited for the cliff divers to begin their show. Four times that week, he had already been and watched, but for him, there was the hope that one day one of them would misjudge the leap and crack their skulls open on the jagged craggy rocks.

Shortly after getting the hell out of Havana, having witnessed the murder of his partner and the death of his dreams, Station Master had wasted little time in securing as much money from the accounts that he could. All in all, he had embezzled enough to last him the rest of his natural life and sometime into his unnatural life.

He sipped from the glass of tequila as he listened to the phone. He hated making calls like this, but these were now desperate times.

"Yes," he said. "It was a complete success... Almost one hundred percent conversion rate... No, he didn't make it out." He chuckled and took another sip. "You were right about Jeremiah

Banks... You are always right... Phase 2?" He glanced at the rocks and water and a part of him wanted to dive into it, just to see if he would survive. "Phase 2 is ready? Excellent. I'll start the preparations... Good... Adios."

He hung up, removed the sim card, and casually tossed the phone over the balcony. Looking at the piece of plastic, he held it over the flame of a lit candle. Slowly, it started to melt. When he was satisfied, Station Master tossed it over too.

The lovely señorita sitting next to him looked exquisitely beautiful in that way only a paid escort does. She looked bored and was staring out into the night. Station Master had had many women since arriving, but this one was definitely his favorite. *I must put her on permanent retainer*, he thought and shuddered slightly as a cool breeze came in off of the sea.

"Mi amor," he said, patting her hand, "I'm cold. Why don't you go and get my coat? The heavy one. You wouldn't want me to get sick and die on you?"

The woman started to curse in Español; she was a prized escort, not a serving wench, but she got up anyway and left the table. The old man was paying well enough.

Station Master looked down and saw a large crowd forming on the viewing platform. There was something about the danger of diving into rocky waters that made him feel alive.

A cough brought him out of his reverie. "Gracias, mi vida."

He turned and almost screamed.

Christine stood before him, a noose in her hand.

THE END

Christine Moore will return in Book 2 of the Apocalypse Virus Trilogy

ACKNOWLEDGMENTS:

Thanks to Mapi for pushing me to finish this in the first place, also thanks should be given to my parents for giving me life and making sure I survived for this long. Special mention should go to Severed Press for taking a chance on this book. And to anyone with a dream or desire, thank you for not quitting. The world needs more people like you.

Come and say hi on my social media:
twitter - @RF_Blackstone
facebook - https://www.facebook.com/Blackstone.RF/
By following me you'll be first to know about new books and just the randomness of my mind.

And if you like the book, leave a review. Even if it is just one word, like "Lovely", or "Orgasmic" hell, even "Good" will do. Reviews help authors like me. So be a pal and do it, do it, do it now!

CHECK OUT OTHER GREAT ZOMBIE NOVELS

VACCINATION
by Phillip Tomasso

What if the H7N9 vaccination wasn't just a preventative measure against swine flu?

It seemed like the flu came out of nowhere and yet, in no time at all the government manufactured a vaccination. Were lab workers diligent, or could the virus itself have been man-made? Chase McKinney works as a dispatcher at 9-1-1. Taking emergency calls, it becomes immediately obvious that the entire city is infected with the walking dead. His first goal is to reach and save his two children.

Could the walls built by the U.S.A. to keep out illegal aliens, and the fact the Mexican government could not afford to vaccinate their citizens against the flu, make the southern border the only plausible destination for safety?

ZOMBIE, INC
by Chris Dougherty

"WELCOME! To Zombie, Inc. The United Five State Republic's leading manufacturer of zombie defense systems! In business since 2027, Zombie, Inc. puts YOU first. YOUR safety is our MAIN GOAL! Our many home defense options - from Ze Fence® to Ze Popper® to Ze Shed® - fit every need and every budget. Use Scan Code "TELL ME MORE!" for your FREE, in-home*, no obligation consultation! *Schedule your appointment with the confidence that you will NEVER HAVE TO LEAVE YOUR HOME! It isn't safe out there and we know it better than most! Our sales staff is FULLY TRAINED to handle any and all adversarial encounters with the living and the undead". Twenty-five years after the deadly plague, the United Five State Republic's most successful company, Zombie, Inc., is in trouble. Will a simple case of dwindling supply and lessening demand be the end of them or will Zombie, Inc. find a way, however unpalatable, to survive?

CHECK OUT OTHER GREAT ZOMBIE NOVELS

900 MILES
by S. Johnathan Davis

John is a killer, but that wasn't his day job before the Apocalypse.

In a harrowing 900 mile race against time to get to his wife just as the dead begin to rise, John, a business man trapped in New York, soon learns that the zombies are the least of his worries, as he sees first-hand the horror of what man is capable of with no rules, no consequences and death at every turn.

Teaming up with an ex-army pilot named Kyle, they escape New York only to stumble across a man who says that he has the key to a rumored underground stronghold called Avalon..... Will they find safety? Will they make it to Johns wife before it's too late?

Get ready to follow John and Kyle in this fast paced thriller that mixes zombie horror with gladiator style arena action!

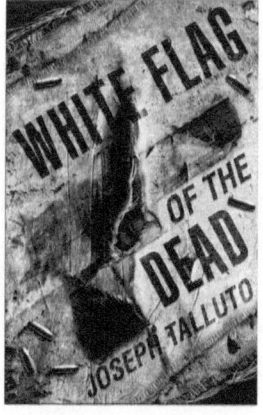

WHITE FLAG OF THE DEAD
by Joseph Talluto

Millions died when the Enillo Virus swept the earth. Millions more were lost when the victims of the plague refused to stay dead, instead rising to slaughter and feed on those left alive. For survivors like John Talon and his son Jake, they are faced with a choice: Do they submit to the dead, raising the white flag of surrender? Or do they find the will to fight, to try and hang on to the last shreds or humanity?

CHECK OUT OTHER GREAT ZOMBIE NOVELS

Z BURBIA
by Jake Bible

Whispering Pines is a classic, quiet, private American subdivision on the edge of Asheville, NC, set in the pristine Blue Ridge Mountains. Which is good since the zombie apocalypse has come to Western North Carolina and really put suburban living to the test!

Surrounded by a sea of the undead, the residents of Whispering Pines have adapted their bucolic life of block parties to scavenging parties, common area groundskeeping to immediate area warfare, neighborhood beautification to neighborhood fortification.

But, even in the best of times, suburban living has its ups and downs what with nosy neighbors, a strict Home Owners' Association, and a property management company that believes the words "strict interpretation" are holy words when applied to the HOA covenants. Now with the zombie apocalypse upon them even those innocuous, daily irritations quickly become dramatic struggles for personal identity, family security, and straight up survival.

ZOMBIE RULES
by David Achord

Zach Gunderson's life sucked and then the zombie apocalypse began.

Rick, an aging Vietnam veteran, alcoholic, and prepper, convinces Zach that the apocalypse is on the horizon. The two of them take refuge at a remote farm. As the zombie plague rages, they face a terrifying fight for survival.

They soon learn however that the walking dead are not the only monsters.

www.ingramcontent.com/pod-product-compliance
Lightning Source LLC
Chambersburg PA
CBHW032002170626
46807CB00006B/2611